THE HORSEMEN
&
THE DERBY MAN

GARY MCCARTHY

The Horsemen & The Derby Man

Paperback Edition

Wolfpack Publishing
6032 Wheat Penny Avenue
Las Vegas, NV 89122
wolfpackpublishing.com

ISBN 978-1-64734-985-1 (paperback) 978-1-64734-984-4 (ebook)

THE HORSEMEN
&
THE DERBY MAN

CHAPTER 1

Post-Civil War—Arizona Territory

Tennessee born and raised Rufus Ballou and his younger sister, Dixie, were sitting in a Flagstaff café on a cold and blustery morning having breakfast while trying to hide their growing impatience. Outside, the air was thick with snow flurries sifting through tall Ponderosa pines and the main street was coated with a glittering patina of ice.

"Where is Houston?" Dixie finally asked. "He knows we agreed to meet here for breakfast and talk about buying horse property."

"I'm still not convinced we should start a new Thoroughbred ranch at this altitude," Ruff said. "Everything up in these mountains is expensive and the snows can get very deep. We'd be cracking thick ice on our horse watering troughs all winter. Also, our line of Thoroughbreds prefer warm weather."

"Yes, but this high altitude would give our horses better wind for running."

Ruff was a tall young man, lean and handsome,

with one ear lobe shot off in a gunfight. Not a man concerned with this minor disfigurement, he offered his impatient sister a smile and shrugged his broad shoulders. "I imagine our big brother was up late gambling last night. Houston's mind was set on winning us enough extra cash to buy that property."

"If we sell just one of the new Thoroughbred foals, we'd have enough to buy the land," Dixie reasoned.

"I know that," Ruff agreed, "but in addition to the land, we'll need quite a bit more to get a ranch built and supplied for the next winter. Horse hay isn't cheap out in Flagstaff. I'm coming to think that this high mountain country is best suited for mules and mustangs."

"We're not far from the Navajo lands," Dixie argued. "They love betting on horse races. And we could travel to Santa Fe and Taos for even bigger money races. In the meantime, I'll find a town job to help put hay in the mangers and food on our table."

"Houston and I can find local work. Your job should be to look after our Thoroughbreds."

"If we buy up here, we can figure it out later," Dixie said. "It will depend on who can find jobs in Flagstaff."

"I imagine that would be Houston and myself," Ruff told her. "The man at the bank said there is always work for freighters and people good at working with livestock."

"We'll do whatever is necessary. We always do. Maybe we can find a few horse races before the heavy snow starts flying and win money."

"That's possible, but we both know the stallions

aren't in racing condition and our mares are all in foal."

"It won't be easy," Dixie admitted. "But I think that we've finally found a place where we can make a fresh start. We've traveled so far since leaving Tennessee and I'm tired of being on the run year after year."

"Me too."

Dixie glanced out the window. "Do you think they are still hunting for us?"

"You mean the Confederates?"

"Who else? The war is over but we've both heard that there's a lot of bitterness and hatred in the South. Killing and raiding, too."

"It'll take decades for things to get right again in the South," Ruff said with a sigh. "And even though the slaves were freed by Lincoln, his assassination changed everything. I don't want to think about what the South used to be before the Civil War and what it must be like now ... what's left of it."

"Me neither." Dixie's eyes clouded. "We had a family and a beautiful horse ranch. Our Tennessee Wildwood Farm was famous for the Thoroughbred blood lines Father created. We had racehorse buyers begging for our horses and a life we'll never see the likes of again."

"I know. I try to put it all behind me."

She looked right into her brother's eyes. "And you can actually do that?"

"Not often, but a little more and more."

Ruff used his fork to push around a small piece tortilla in a hardening jell of egg yolk. "Dixie, we lost our father and most of our brothers in that war. We lost a life we loved … but we have to move on, and I admire this country out in the West. Not all of it, of course, but a lot is nothing short of spectacular. I like the clear, sharp air and the long views we have of mountain ranges and huge, open valleys. It's a place where we can put down roots and start all over again, leaving hatred and death far behind."

"Yeah," Dixie reminded her brother again, "unless there are some still hunting us for what happened the day we left Tennessee."

They both fell into a troubled silence. Ruff finally reached across the table and laid his big hand on Dixie's arm. It troubled him to see her so worried about their uncertain future. They were as close as two peas in a pod and the best horsemen of the Ballou family.

Like Ruff, Dixie was tall, slender and attractive, but not a young woman who anyone would mistake for being outright beautiful. Her eyes were dark brown like those of their Cherokee mother and so was her long black hair. Her skin was deeply tanned, and the backs of her hands were almost the color of hickory because she spent so much time riding and exercising the Ballou horses alongside her brother.

Nine o'clock came and went and so did the breakfast, but Houston was still missing. The owner of the little Mexican café came to their table. "More tortillas?" he asked with a wide smile. "Hot with my wife's special salsa."

Ruff grinned. "Nada, Jose. We are waiting for our big brother."

"He's never on time for anything," Dixie explained.

"I see him going to the post office early this morning. He was whistling and looked happy."

"Well, that's good news," Dixie said, "but we're not happy waiting here all morning for him to show up."

"I could fix you both a little something stronger than coffee," Jose suggested, with the wink of his eye. "Something that will make spending time here much more pleasant."

Ruff knew what the man was suggesting, and he wasn't ready for a potent mix of tequila and cocoa the way that Jose Escobar often made for his favored customers.

"Here comes Houston now," Ruff said, pointing out the window.

"See," Jose said, "I told you he looked happy."

"He must have won a fair amount of money last night in the saloon," Dixie said. "Thank heavens he didn't lose any. We need every dollar we can get to buy that property just west of town."

"It's a very good place," Jose said in a serious tone. "It was once a fine ranch until we had a drought and the most of our wells went dry for two years."

"I hadn't heard about that," Ruff said, suddenly concerned. "How long ago was this drought?"

"It was around the start the war," Jose said. "But the snow and rain have been good this year."

"It could happen again," Dixie fretted.

"We'd have to dig large stock ponds to conserve the snow melt," Ruff said. "It's not an issue if the price of the property is right. Also, there's a big, flat meadow we can develop into a racetrack."

"There's no perfect property," Dixie agreed. "We've seen a lot of country since leaving Tennessee and none of it had everything. At least here in the Arizona Territory the land is cheap."

"It is," Ruff agreed. "But I just can't stop worrying about this high altitude and hard winters."

Ruff was going to say more, but Jose said, "Excuse me, but your brother will be hungry, and I will bring him a plate of hot tortillas, eggs and beans."

"Good," Ruff said, easing back in his chair.

Houston made his entry into the café like he made every entry . . . with a swagger and a broad, confident smile. "My oh my!" he boomed. "What a night and what a morning! I have some wonderful news."

"How much did you win?" Dixie blurted.

Houston was not as tall as Ruff, but he was still well over six feet and stockier. His handsome looks made him a magnet for pretty women, and he was not shy about using his natural charm to steal their hearts. Yet, Ruff knew that his brother was a true Southern gentleman. Unfortunately, Houston had a quick temper and a tendency to occasionally drink too much and get into trouble but, somehow, he always managed to get through it.

"I have two pieces of great news for you this morning," Houston announced, dropping into a chair. "Three, really."

"All since we had dinner last night?" Dixie asked.

"Yes!" Houston's dark eyes danced. "First, I won four hundred dollars at the poker table last night."

"Four hundred?" Ruff asked. "How ..."

"You know that gambler that works the tables

at the saloon? The loud-mouthed and uncouth big man named Rio who brags that he was once a famous Texas Ranger?"

"Yeah," Ruff said, frowning. "His name is Rio and he intimidates most men."

"Well, not me!" Houston said, banging his fist down on the table so hard the plates and cutlery jumped.

Both Ruff and Dixie noticed their older brother's knuckles, which were bloody. Ruff spoke first asking the question that was on their minds. "Did you whip him?"

"Oh yeah," Houston said proudly. "He was up on me over a hundred dollars and had cleaned out a couple of other players when I finally caught him cheating at cards. I grabbed his sleeve, shook loose a couple of hide-out cards and then I grabbed his thumb and broke it like stick. I did it so fast Rio jerked back with a howl and more cards spilled out of his other sleeve!"

"But what about your bloody knuckles?"

"He was a helluva fighter," Houston admitted. "I went right after him and finally managed to get him on the floor and almost beat his brains out."

"You sure messed up those hands," Dixie said, her brow furrowed with worry. "Did you break any knuckles?"

"I don't think so," Houston said, inspecting his fists as he slowly clenched and unclenched them. "But anyway, I got back my money and everything he'd brought to the game. Before I was dragged off Rio, I broke a couple more of his fingers on both his hands, so he won't be cheating at cards for a long,

long time. Maybe never again."

Dixie shook her head. "He's probably going to try and get even."

"I expect he might," Houston agreed, smile fading. "Sooner or later, I might have to kill him.

"But now I have some even better news."

"Let's hear it," Ruff said.

Houston gushed, "I'm gonna get engaged to be married to Miss Olivia Jensen!"

"What!"

"You heard me."

"You proposed marriage to that woman?" Dixie asked in disbelief. "Were you even a little bit sober?"

"Hell, yes! If we're going to settle down here and build a horse ranch, I figured it was time to find a good wife."

Dixie gently shook her head. "Houston, you can't be serious."

"Oh, but I am!" He threw back his head and laughed. "Miss Jensen is beautiful, and her father has money that could come in handy." Houston winked. "If you know what I mean."

"Missus Jensen is already married."

"I know. I know," Houston said, "but she can get an annulment. You see, her husband is uh, uh ... well, he ain't able to do what a man needs to do so they can have kids."

"Houston!" Dixie cried with exasperation. "She actually told you that!"

"She did and I believe her. She doesn't love Arthur Jensen. Never did."

"Then why did she even marry him?" Ruff

demanded.

"She just did and then she found out he really likes other men." Houston's cheeks reddened with embarrassment.

Ruff covered his face and groaned. Then he looked up at his brother. "I can't believe what I'm hearing. Have you gone entirely mad!"

"I have not," he said, anger flashing in his eyes. "I've been watching that woman and admiring her since we rode into Flagstaff. She's beautiful, smart and educated. And I could tell that she was admiring me. So, one day we got to talking . . . just real nice in front of everyone and then we started talking more kinda in private and one thing led to another and ..."

"Stop it!" Dixie ordered. "This is whole conversation is ridiculous."

"Not to me it isn't," Houston said stubbornly. "I'm gonna buy her an engagement ring. She said she would help us build a horse ranch and ..."

"Brother, that's not going to work."

"It has to work," Houston said solemnly. "Olivia says she might be in trouble with that cheatin' gambler, Rio. Turns out they … well, they were together before I showed up."

Dixie stood up. "I think I'm about to need some fresh air."

"Hold up," Ruff told his sister. "We all need to have a calm—but serious—talk."

Houston's eyes flashed with anger. "What the hell! I thought you'd both be real happy for me and Olivia. And Ruff, someday you're going to fall in love and propose marriage and maybe I won't like the woman you pick … but I'll keep that to myself and act happy. I'll do it because I love you and I'd never break this family peace."

Dixie took a deep breath and asked, "What was the third piece of great news you had to tell us?"

"Not sure I want to tell either of you anything more after the way you've both just acted."

"Come on," Ruff urged. "What is it?"

Reluctantly, Houston dragged out a letter that he obviously already torn open. "This is from our old neighbors back in Tennessee. The Petersons. They say that two families of carpetbaggers have set up house at our Wildwood Farm and they mean to get title to it, but a judge ruled against them … an old southern gentleman who somehow kept his gavel and honesty. The letter also says that, if we want our Tennessee horse ranch back, we have to return and go to court in Chattanooga with some papers, which we did take before we left on the run. He said Wildwood Farm is in bad shape but that in a year we could make it just as nice and showy as it was before the war."

"And *that's* good news?" Ruff asked quietly.

"Sure it is!"

Houston looked from Dixie to Ruff. "All we have to do is go back and legally settle ownership in our favor. Then we can either live at Wildwood Farm permanently or sell it for a whole bunch of money. Money we could use in Arizona to buy a damn fine ranch. That way we could start off in the West as a prosperous family instead of a collection of poor Southerners living from hand to mouth."

Dixie slowly sat down again. "We're not penniless, Houston. We've got some very valuable Thoroughbreds, remember?"

"Yes, but with a bundle of cash we could immediately buy the things that we need to set up a first rate horse ranch without having to scrimp for years and take side jobs to make ends meet."

Dixie took a deep breath and looked at her two fine brothers, finally saying, "You are all the family I have left now. Have you both entirely forgotten how we left Tennessee on the run from the Confederacy for that shootout we were in where we forced to kill Captain Denton and a couple of our own soldiers?"

"No," Houston said quietly. "But Jefferson Davis and the Confederacy don't exist anymore. Our father had to defend himself and our last few Thoroughbred horses. Captain Denton was crazed from battles and he would have had us all hanged or shot ... if Pa hadn't killed him first."

"And just who would our witnesses be to that act of self-defense?" Ruff asked pointedly. "*Who* would testify for us now that the North has taken everything over and the carpetbaggers are running the South?"

Houston opened his mouth, then clamped it shut.

"We need to talk about buying land here for our horse ranch," Dixie told her brothers. "But I don't think this is the time or place for it."

"Nor do I," Ruff agreed.

Houston was angry. "Alright then, we'll talk later. But I am marrying Olivia Jensen. And if she won't be welcomed by my family, I'll take her back to

Tennessee and we'll fight and reclaim our property. I'll run the damned carpetbaggers off and rebuild what our father gave his life to defend!"

Dixie sighed. "Houston," she said quietly, "you are a fine brother and I love you dearly but you sure can be a stubborn fool when it comes to women." She left the room.

"Excuse me," Ruff said, going after his sister and catching her just outside. "Dixie, let's let him get some sleep before we talk again."

"He seems as if he's made up his mind and he won't change it. You know how he is when he gets something set in his mind. He's like an old Missouri mule."

"We can't stop him from going all the way back to Tennessee," Ruff reminded her. "But maybe we can figure a way to get rid of Missus Olivia Jensen."

"Any ideas?"

"Not yet," Ruff admitted. "But perhaps the best thing we can do is to take her out to look at that rundown ranch we're thinking of buying and see how she reacts. She doesn't strike me as the pioneering type of woman. I think she's accustomed to money and an easy life and she has no idea of what it would mean to live away from town."

"I pray you're right. I've seen the woman and she is a beauty, but she's legally married! Houston's talk of an annulment is crazy."

"I don't know how the law works in this new territory," Ruff said, "but even you would have to admit that it'd be a real test of Olivia's love for our brother if she went through with the annulment, married Houston and stuck it out on a horse ranch."

Dixie shook her head with exasperation. "I can't believe that she's been fooling around with that former Texas Ranger named Rio! Is she crazy?"

"I don't know," Ruff confessed. "But being married to a man who prefers other men would make a lot of women desperate to figure out an escape from their marriage."

"I understand that, but my concern is for what's left of our family. Houston has a foolish romantic streak and it brings him grief. Remember how he went to Washington after a woman spy for the Confederacy and almost died in their prison?"

"I remember."

"This could turn out even worse. Houston isn't ready for marriage."

"I'm afraid you're right."

Ruff took his sister's arm and steered her toward their hotel. He was thinking that everything in their lives had been turned upside down. They'd fled Tennessee with revenge-filled southerners on their heels. They'd barely survived Comanche and Kiowa warriors on the Plains and thieves and killers in Texas and New Mexico. Somehow, they'd managed to bring the very last of their famed Thoroughbreds all the way out to this new Arizona Territory where tall Ponderosa, pinion and juniper pines made the air taste almost as sweet as peppermint candy.

And now this mess with Houston had fouled up everything. If he got himself married to a woman he hardly knew, Ruff figured that would be a disaster. Rio, the card cheat and former Texas Ranger, was the kind of man who would never rest without taking revenge for his humiliation and savage beating. Ruff suspected that man, broken fingers and all, could be downright deadly.

And finally, if Houston got really angry and returned to Wildwood Farm and the reconstruction South, he might very well not only fail to regain ownership of their former home and land, but he might be hanged as a traitor and murderer.

What in the devil else could go wrong?

CHAPTER 2

Flagstaff banker George Morrison was handling the sale of the ranch property, and he was not pleased as he glared at Ruff and Dixie from behind his desk.

"Yesterday, you told me to work up the papers on that property and we more or less agreed on a price. It's great buy! You'd be getting five hundred acres of forest and meadowland, a nice house and barns plus a year around creek. It has fencing and …"

"We heard that the creek went dry a few years ago during the drought and the well isn't reliable," Ruff said, interrupting Morrison. "And as for a price … well, we've not settled on it yet."

"It's $900.00," Morrison snapped. "I told you the seller wouldn't go a cent lower."

"We want to go out and see it again," Dixie insisted. "And we're taking Olivia Jensen."

The banker blinked with surprise. "What on earth has Mrs. Jensen to do with buying the property?"

Ruff shifted uneasily in his chair. "We'd rather not say."

George Morrison rolled his eyes, straightened his tie and said in a curt tone of voice, "And I don't really think I want to know what the woman is up to next. I will say this, she's likely the prettiest woman between San Francisco and Santa Fe, but she's a mountain of trouble. Always has been and always will be, and if you are thinking of asking her father for some of the money to buy that property, I think maybe we ought to just forget the whole thing."

"We're paying our own way without any help from anyone," Ruff told the banker. "But we want to see the property and go inside the house this time. Check out the well to see how deep it really is. Look closer at the barn, corrals and fencing. See how much salable timber there is on the land."

"There's a lot of prime timber," Morrison argued. "The timber alone is worth ... oh, two, maybe even three hundred delivered at the sawmill."

"We're not in the lumbering business," Dixie told the banker.

Morrison leaned back in his chair. "You do know that Olivia Jensen is a married woman."

"We do."

"And that her husband is a very fine man and highly respected in this part of the country. If you dishonor Mr. Jensen, there will be repercussions. You would create a scandal of huge proportions and a lot of ill will."

"We don't think it will come to that," Ruff answered.

There was a long moment of silence before Morrison sighed then reached into his desk drawer and found a key. "This opens the front door to the ranch house. Look around and I'm sure you'll see that it's in poor shape and in need of repairs. It's been abandoned for a while and …"

"Thank you," Dixie said, cutting the man off and coming to her feet.

"Lock the door when you leave the ranch house and bring me back the key first chance you get. I may have another interested party. That place is one hell of a good buy!"

"Sure it is," Ruff said, figuring it was a bluff to push them into making an offer.

Ruff, Houston and Dixie decided that the best way to leave town with Olivia and avoid scandal was to rent a closed carriage, and they were fortunate to find one at the livery stable.

Without wasting a day, and much to Dixie's displeasure, they put her inside with Olivia and left Flagstaff on a back street. The property was only about four miles away and the weather was clear but quite cold. To hear Olivia talk as they rolled along, you'd have thought it was a hundred miles from Flagstaff.

"My goodness but this ranch is far out!" she exclaimed over and over as she peered through the window. "However can we manage in such a remote place!"

"It's not what we'd call remote," Dixie replied with ice in her voice. "If you put your mind to it, you could walk from the ranch to the town in an hour."

"Why would anyone ever walk out here in this …

this wilderness? I would expect a carriage at least as nice as this one."

"How much do you know about horses?"

"Nothing at all. My father had someone give me a few riding lessons when I was a girl … but I hated it and stopped."

"You ever clean a corral?"

"Whatever for?"

Dixie had heard enough and didn't trust herself to speak a word for the rest of the short ride out to the abandoned ranch.

When they drove into the yard covered with a light snowfall, Houston hurried over to the carriage. "There it is, darlin'!"

Olivia stuck her pretty head out of the window and gasped, "Oh my, it looks so … so dark and sad!"

"Just needs a little elbow grease!"

Olivia fell back in her seat for a moment with her eyes wide and scared looking.

"Come on," Houston urged, nearly pulling her out of the carriage. "Try to imagine what it will look like after we fix things up a bit."

Once they crossed the ranch yard, things didn't get any better. When they entered the front room, mice scrambled across a flagstone floor, shot up the chimney and dived into dark corners and crevasses. Olivia cried out in alarm and hugged Houston's neck as if she were about to be devoured by a wild animal.

"Just needs some cleaning out," he said, knocking cobwebs away as they made their way from room to dark and dusty room.

"I don't know if I can do this," Olivia whined.

"Houston, I just don't!"

"It'll clean up nice and pretty. Just take a week or two."

"Years," Olivia whispered, a shaky hand passing over her face.

Dixie pinned her oldest brother with her eyes and gave him a slow shake of her head, but Houston ignored her.

"Tell you what, Livy," he said, trying to sound encouraging. "Let's go outside and look at the yard. You'll see the potential. I know it's different from what you're used to, but we could make this a showplace."

"A showplace!" Olivia cried. "For what, a hog farm!"

Dixie had to fight to keep silent and from the look on Ruff's face, he was having the same struggle.

So, they went outside, and things were better. The big barn was well constructed and would hold a lot of hay and there were six good stalls inside. There was at least a ton of meadow hay in the loft, but Ruff figured it would be moldy and in need of being thrown out or burned in the yard. There were other corrals and a few sheds and a nice flagstone patio under a towering red-barked pine tree.

"Look at the pretty squirrels up in that tree," Houston said, taking Olivia's arm and pointing. "You ever seen such handsome little critters? Why, they got pointy, silver-tipped ears. I swear I never seen the likes of 'em!"

"Don't tell me you would expect to shoot them for eating," Olivia said fearfully. "They look like tree rats to me."

Houston's smile died. "Well," he said, pointing the ground. "There is a lot of game on this land. These bigger round turds are from elk while the smaller round ones are deer droppings."

"In our yard, how charming," Olivia whispered, seeming to look for something to sit down upon and rest.

Houston was nothing if not persistent. "I can tell you that these tall pines will sing a sweet song when the wind blows, and their branches will hold onto snow and make everything beautiful in the wintertime."

"Houston, dear. I have to ... well, do my business. Where?"

"Pick a tree to get behind," Dixie said with wicked satisfaction. "Any wide tree out here will do nicely."

For the first time, Olivia Jensen shot Dixie a withering glance. "I'm not about to drop my dress and drawers behind a damned tree!"

"Well, there's some Manzanita brush over there, but an elk might be resting in among them and get after you. And with your dress down to your ankles, it'd be hard to move fast enough to escape."

Olivia glare turned pure poison.

"Look at the stream," Ruff said.

"It's almost running dry," Dixie replied. "Not nearly enough for our needs."

"Maybe the well will be good."

But it wasn't. They lowered the bucket a way before it splashed and when they brought it up, the water was muddy.

They spent an hour at the property and by then Olivia Jensen was throwing a fit. Actually, this was exactly what Ruff and Dixie had hoped for and expected. Houston's expression had gone from hopeful and excited, to downright stormy.

"Just took one hour to get this issue straightened out," Dixie whispered to Ruff. "I can think it's safe to say that Houston has seen the real Olivia and it's not much to his liking."

"I agree. Let's go back to town and buy this place. We can turn it into something special."

"Even with the issue of water being scarce and the well being muddy?" Dixie asked anxiously.

"I think so," Ruff replied. "When we get rid of Olivia we can talk to Houston and about where we'd put the holding ponds."

"This is awfully rocky land," Dixie warned. "Digging ponds would be the devil of our time. Pick and shovel work, I'd say."

"Maybe we'd have enough money to get someone to bring in a team of draft horses and a drag to help scoop out a pond for spring runoff," Ruff offered. "We'll figure out something. Anything worth doing is difficult, given what's left of our Ballou family."

"I wouldn't argue you on that, Brother."

Ruff was about to say something when he caught sight of a movement in the trees down by the ranch house. It wasn't a deer or an elk because he'd seen white but ...

"Take cover!" he shouted, seeing Rio step out from behind a big pine. Both of the man's ruined hands were partially bandaged but that didn't prevent him from bringing up a Winchester rifle and opening fire on Houston.

Trouble was, Houston spun sideways but Olivia froze and took his intended bullet.

They all saw the blood explode from Olivia's large bosom an instant before she fell onto a bed of wet pine needles.

Houston was the best gunman of the Ballou men, fast as a striking rattlesnake on the draw and deadly accurate. But Rio was standing a good hundred feet away and had now opened fire on all of them, levering shots and unleashing bullets despite his broken fingers.

Houston took a shot in the leg that twisted him completely around. He grunted in pain and fell with his gun bucking in his hand. Ruff knew the chance of him hitting Rio with a revolver at this distance wasn't good, but they hadn't thought to bring a rifle.

Ruff unleashed three bullets, then he saw Rio's head explode, painting his brains against the trunk of a big, red-barked Ponderosa pine. Ruff turned and ran back to his brother who was on the ground trying to hold his leg and staunch the bleeding with Dixie at his side.

"Olivia is dead, and Houston needs a doctor," Dixie said with surprising calmness.

"He'd bleed out before we could get back to town," Ruff said. "We need to take care of Houston ourselves."

"Well, let's get him to the house."

Houston was heavy and it took a real effort to get him down to the abandoned ranch house. They laid him on a dusty old couch.

"Bandages!" Ruff shouted. "The bullet looks to have passed right through his upper leg."

"Major blood vessels?" Dixie asked, looking frantically around for any clean cloth to use.

"I don't know yet."

"I'm going to make it," Houston gritted. "Gawdamn that Rio! If he wasn't dead already, I'd kill him all over again!"

"Oh, he's dead alright." Ruff looked to his sister. "Only clean cloth I can think of is on Olivia. You'd better go get that dress and her drawers, Sister."

Dixie was grim faced but knew her brother was right. "I'll be right back," she said, running out of the door.

"Oh my gawd!" Houston said, "I've sure messed this whole thing up and poor Olivia didn't need to die."

"She didn't suffer. Olivia was dead before she hit the pine needles," Ruff told his brother.

"If I hadn't tried to get her to agree to live in a place like this, she'd still be alive."

"Maybe so," Ruff replied. "But sooner or later a man like Rio would have done Olivia and her poor husband harm."

Houston nodded. "I think it was your bullet that hit him in the head."

"I think it was yours," Ruff replied, pretty sure that was true.

"Don't matter none," Houston whispered. "You think the bullet shattered my leg bone?"

"I do not."

"Good."

"You still think we ought to buy this place."

"No," Ruff answered tightly. "This has put a curse on it for us. I was worried anyway about the water and how hard the winters can get up in this high country."

"Yeah," Houston gritted. "But by the size of those elk turds, I'll bet we'd never had wanted for fresh meat."

"Probably right about that," Ruff told his brother just before Dixie returned with poor Olivia's dress and drawers.

Houston moaned as they tore the clothing into strips and wrapped the wound.

"Let's get him out to the carriage."

"We're not leaving Olivia here," Houston said between clenched teeth. "You can leave Rio, but not Olivia."

"Understood," Ruff told his brother.

Once Houston and Olivia were in the carriage, they hurried back to Rio's body. They propped the former Texas Ranger up against the same pine that was decorated with his brains. They took his weapons and ammunition and didn't bother to empty his pockets. If Rio was carrying cash, whoever found him could take it as compensation for burying the man from Texas.

"Helluva day," Houston said that night in the hotel as a crowd milled around the mortician's office to see a half undressed and but not so beautiful Mrs. Olivia Jensen. "I wonder how her husband is handling this?"

"I hope to never find out," Ruff muttered. "As

soon as we can, we're leaving this place and never looking back."

"Where do we go next?" Dixie asked quietly.

"We keep moving west. We'll find a better place. A place with more reliable water and grass. A place where the winters are easier on our Thoroughbreds and where we won't find trouble and trouble won't be able to find us."

"I'm beginning to think there is no such place," Houston said bitterly, hoisting a bottle of whiskey that he was well on his way to drinking dry.

Ruff thought about that and wondered if it that was true. They'd come so far and gone through so much since Tennessee. They were just horsemen looking for a peaceful new beginning. But peaceful new beginnings didn't seem to want to come their way.

CHAPTER 3

It had taken almost a week for Houston's leg wound to heal well enough that he could travel on horseback. During that time, things had been unpleasant and even difficult for what was left of the Ballou family. The town went out of their way to avoid them and most seemed to think that they were solely responsible for the death of lovely Olivia Jensen.

"They look at me like I'm evil," Dixie said. "I've tried to act friendly, but they shun me, and I know they hate the three of us."

"I don't blame them," Ruff said quietly, "because they don't know the true circumstances. They probably think that Houston seduced Mrs. Jensen… not imagining that it was the other way around with not only our brother, but with that former Texas Ranger. That's what got her killed and almost got us all shot dead."

"Why did she do that to Houston and Rio?"

"I don't know," Ruff admitted. "But I believe

Rio's first bullet was really meant for Olivia and his second for Houston. He'd have sensed that Houston was the most dangerous and he had the rifle range to his advantage. Dixie, I think we're all three lucky to still be alive."

"I just want to leave this town and never come back. The weather is turning bad and it's freezing hard every night. There's a storm coming. I can feel it in my bones, and we need to get down from these high mountains. Our mares are in various late stages of pregnancy. We need to settle in a better place, Ruff. And soon."

"I know. If Houston is up to it, we'll head west first thing in the morning."

"He should travel in a buckboard," Dixie said. "But I know him, and he won't allow that."

"Then he'll ride High Man and I'll ride the younger, more spirited High Fire," Ruff told his sister. "And maybe by tomorrow night we'll be off this mountain."

Dixie worried that Houston's leg wound might get infected or break open on horseback. She also fretted that someone was still following them for a reward that was reputed to be offered for their arrest by the Union Army or a sizable bounty issued by former Confederates. Most of all, she was worried that Houston might actually leave go back to Tennessee in the foolish hope that he could regain title to Wildwood Farm.

"I wonder if we'll have to go all the way to California and the Pacific Ocean before we at last find a settling down place for our prized Thoroughbreds."

"I don't know," Ruff said honestly. "But I expect when we do find the right place, we'll know it."

On their last night in Flagstaff they were hit by a fierce snowstorm. The wind howled and the snow piled up until it was even with the town's rickety boardwalks. When Ruff left his bed to join Dixie for breakfast in the hotel dining room, the place was filled with people and everyone was talking about the weather.

"I've seen a storm up here bring in five foot of snow," their waiter said as he brought them breakfast. "Five feet in one night! We might get snowed in. Wouldn't surprise me at all."

Ruff and Dixie ate in anxious silence, both focused on how they were going to get off this mountain. Finally, Ruff growled, "We should have left last week."

"How could we have with Houston laid up? He lost a lot of blood."

"We could have insisted he ride in the bed of a buckboard. We could have easily sold the buckboard when Houston was better mended and able to ride."

"Well, we didn't so there's no use in thinking about it now," Dixie reasoned. "We'll just have to wait until the weather clears and hurry off this mountain."

"Yeah. Only good thing is that we didn't spend all our money on property. If we'd have done that then we'd be in a hell of a mess."

The weather cleared just as fast as it had turned bad the night before. Next morning, Ruff and Dixie saddled High Man and his son High Fire, who was the future of their foundation line of race horses, along with a mare for Dixie to ride and packed the basic provisions they needed for the next few days.

"You sure you can do this without busting open that wound?" Dixie asked her older brother as they prepared to mount up outside the stable. "If you get tossed or High Man slips and falls on ice and your leg wound breaks open, you could bleed to death right out on the road and there wouldn't be much that Ruff or I could do to save you."

"I'll be fine. I'm a Ballou and I don't get tossed by horses."

"Oh, you can say that, but I've seen you get thrown more than once back in Tennessee while breaking horses."

"And you've seen Ruff tossed as well," Houston said a little defensively. "Just not as often."

When they rode down Flagstaff's main street past the cemetery, they saw two fresh snow-covered grave mounds. Not side by side, but not far from each other. Rio's grave was marked by a small, hastily made wooden cross while Olivia's already had a fine marble headstone.

"This town just wasn't good for us," Dixie said as they passed the cemetery. "Not from the start."

"We'll find a better place soon," Ruff promised.

"After we do, I'm headed for Tennessee," Houston vowed. "I'm going to get Wildwood Farm back or die trying."

Ruff didn't answer. Maybe Houston was just talking out of bitterness. Maybe not. They'd face that when the time came. Houston was a man who made quick and often bad decisions. To Ruff's way of thinking, rushing back to Tennessee was like racing for the gallows or a firing squad and it was a damn shame Houston couldn't figure that out. Ever since Houston had lost his love and Confederate spy, Molly O'Day, his life had turned dark and dangerous. It was like he didn't much care if he lived or died and while he'd always been adventurous and reckless, he was now taking those characteristics to a new and alarming level.

All that morning and in the face of growing thunderheads promising another big storm, the horsemen hurried up a snow-covered road that wound its way higher and higher into the mountains. In the early afternoon they passed a faded wooden sign nailed high up on a tall pine that proclaimed:

CONTINENTAL DIVIDE, elevation 8,000 feet

By then the Ballou mares were struggling. The snow had not melted, and they had been following what was probably a stagecoach's fresh wheel tracks. The mares walked single file in the deep, narrow tracks, attempting to make their movements easier. In the thin, freezing air, the Thoroughbred mares walked with their heads down, warm streams of breath pumping from their nostrils.

"Now that we've crossed the Continental Divide, we'll be dropping down fast from this altitude," Houston said, pointing off into the western horizon. "My guess is we'll not have to ride more than fifty miles and then we'll be in the high desert country where it'll be above freezing."

"These horses won't make it another fifty miles today," Dixie fretted. She squinted into the western sun. "Way up ahead, I think I saw the stagecoach we've been following the last few days."

Ruff nodded. "It seems to be moving off this mountain awfully damned fast."

"Yeah," Dixie agreed. "That's what I'm thinking. I can't imagine why a driver would force his team to gallop downhill on an icy footing."

"Maybe he knows something we don't."

"I hope so."

"We should look for a cabin and corrals to hole up for the night," Ruff told them. "I spotted a cabin and barn back up in the forest not too far ahead."

"I pray that it's a way station or a place to shelter for the night. It's going to be really cold up here in the pines tonight."

"We'll do all right," Houston told them. "We didn't come all the way from Tennessee to freeze to death."

"Amen to that," Ruff said with a tight smile.

The cabin at the edge of the pine forest took in travelers. It was owned by a friendly and hardworking man and his wife and they had a good, weather-tight barn with grass hay for sale.

"Put them blooded racing horses up in the barn, toss 'em hay and then come on in for a hot meal the missus has waitin' for you!" the owner shouted against the driving wind. "Given how many horses you have and there's three of you ... it'll cost five dollars for the night, but you don't want to be caught in a blizzard if another one comes through."

"Five dollars for feeding us and all our horses seems fair," Houston replied, paying the man.

Soon, the Ballou family enjoyed a hot meal and there was a room for sleeping all to themselves with reasonably clean blankets.

"If the weather doesn't go completely bad, you'll be down off this mountain and into the pinion pine and juniper country by tomorrow tonight," their host promised. "Just take it slow and careful because the road gets real steep and slippery this time of year after you pass to the north of Bill Williams Mountain."

"Where does it take us?"

"When you get down outa the Ponderosa pines, you travel a few miles and then there's a fork ... in fact it's called Ash Fork. You can turn directly north and you'll wind up on the South Rim of the Grand Canyon, or west and head for the Colorado River country which is about a hundred miles farther on, or you can turn south toward Prescott. There are a few towns along the way."

"What's in Prescott?" Ruff asked.

"There's Fort Whipple ... the new Army fort located on Granite Creek, along with the governor's mansion and the capitol buildings. But Yuma is fighting for the new capitol and nobody knows if they can get that done ... but they might. Lot more people live in Yuma than Prescott. Anyway, everything in Prescott is under construction but people are flocking to our first territorial capital."

"What about their winters?" Dixie asked.

"It can snow in Prescott, but nothing like up here."

"Then why are you settled in these high mountains?"

The man snugged up in his heavy leather and sheepskin lined coat. He wore a woolen stocking cap pulled right down over his ears. "We're an overnight stop for the stagecoach and other travelers some of whom are going all the way to California. We do a pretty good business year around and we like this tall pine country. In the spring, summer and fall I log timber and hunt deer and elk, which are plentiful. I sell the timber and smoke the venison for feeding our many guests. I have plans to build a small hotel and café using the lumber right off our homestead, and we've a good spring with plenty of clear drinking water."

"That's a lot of reasons to stay," Dixie agreed.

"Yeah, it is. But someday we might just decide to head on down to Prescott and see if we can find ourselves another homestead. As a body gets older, it has less tolerance for the cold and your joints get stiff and hurtful. Still, we work hard and the money here is damned good."

"Well, best of luck to whatever you and the missus do," Ruff told the couple. "Maybe our trails will cross again someday."

"You never can tell. There are a lot of ex-Confederates in this new Arizona Territory. A whole lot of them live down in Yuma. I can tell you people hail from the South. Just be careful about your talk among strangers. The war may be over, but the anger and bitterness between the northerners and southerners still burns hot, even way out here in Arizona."

"We'll remember that," Ruff promised as the man waved and then hurried back inside his warm cabin.

About noon they stopped for a breather. "That must be the high desert country," Ruff said, standing up in his stirrups and surveying the vast country that unfolded to the west. As far as the eye could see the land ahead was dotted with a sea of grayish green juniper and pinion pine and spiked with old volcano domes.

Ruff pulled his wool coat tighter. There was a sharp wind sweeping directly into their faces and the air was remarkably clear yet biting. He glanced sideways at Houston whose face was pale not only from the cold but from pain.

"You doin' okay, Brother?"

"I'll make it. Be glad to get down lower where maybe the wind isn't so bitterly cold."

"Me too," Ruff replied. "This sure is a change from Tennessee."

"Just what I was thinkin'," Houston gritted.

Ruff's mind ran back to Tennessee. The fall colors would be like a splash of sunset across the hills and valleys right now. Magnolias losing their blossoms and the dogwood as red as cherries. There would be fat turkeys calling in the woods, squirrels frantically gathering up nuts for the winter and brightly colored birds on the wing.

So different out here, Ruff thought as his restless mind kept shifting back to the rolling, blue grass country of his birth. It seemed like only yesterday when his life and that of his father and brothers had gone from a near paradise to blazing hell because of the Civil War. Ruff had no idea if the Union Army had actually pillaged and destroyed his family's mansion and fields ... but that seemed a real and likely possibility. General Sherman and his army had pushed through the South like a giant's sickle, leaving nothing and destroying everything in its miles-wide swath of misery and destruction.

Ruff forced his mind back to the land that stretched far into the horizon. Arizona Territory. And although he would never favor another country more dearly than the lush and heavily forested Tennessee, he had to admit to a growing admiration for the rugged openness of the American West. Despite the snow and cold, the sharp scent of wet sagebrush was strong and as invigorating as a medicine wagon huckster's tonic.

Could they finally find a place to build a horse ranch in this new territory worthy of the Ballou name? Just then a hard and sudden gust of cold wind almost blew off Ruff's hat and he clamped it down tight. He tightened up his coat collar and whispered a small but fervent prayer.

"Dear Mother of Cherokee blood, Father of honor and strength and Brothers gone way too soon, I wish you were here to see what the future holds for the last of our Ballou family. We've lost almost everything except High Man and his son, High Fire, plus a few of our best brood mares. We have suffered greatly trying to find a new home ... and peace. So, despite the uncertainties and dangers that lie ahead, we have

reason to be both grateful and hopeful. Just help us find a place to begin again. And let our misguided Confederate enemies hound us no more. Lord, protect us and what we have left. Amen."

Dixie rode up to join him and instantly read his troubled thoughts. "I expect we both know that this land will never match our old home in Tennessee, but it is beautiful in its own vast and mostly empty way."

"Once again I saw that stagecoach we've been tracking. I might be wrong, but it looked like it had overturned on the road down farther this steep mountainside."

"It was moving way too fast," Dixie said. "I sure hope it didn't turn over and kill the horses."

"What about the passengers?" Ruff asked with a wry smile.

"You know I always favor horses over people."

"Yes, I do." Ruff squinted hard. "I believe that stagecoach really did overturn."

"I guess we'll find out soon enough," Houston mused. "We can pick up the pace a bit."

"We can't push the mares any harder," Ruff told them.

He was the most knowledgeable of the Ballou horsemen and his opinion was final when it came to the welfare of their two prized racing stallions and the mares. "Our horses are worn down and it was a hard climb up to the Continental Divide and now down this steep mountain."

Both Dixie and Houston nodded in understanding with their eyes straining to figure out what it was that awaited out on the ice and mud-slick road.

"That stagecoach would be moving if they weren't in serious trouble," Dixie said quietly.

"Hell of a place to overturn," Ruff added. "Way out here on a lonely mountainside road with a freezing night ahead."

"We can't waste much time helping whoever is in trouble," Dixie warned. "We just can't do it in this weather and risk losing any of our horses."

"I know. I know." Ruff's boot heels lightly touched the flanks of the stallion and they continued down the mountainside at a fast walk.

CHAPTER 4

Darby Buckingham, the Derby Man, lay badly shaken and only semi-conscious while vaguely aware that the stagecoach was tilted far over against a ridge of snow and that he was badly banged up. He'd left Santa Fe nearly a week earlier, hiring his own driver, horses and stagecoach, because he was in a huge hurry. His long-time companion, admirer and lady friend, the voluptuous and lovely Miss Dolly Beavers, had him sent an urgent message pleading for Darby to come to her aid in Prescott. Quite out of character, she had not stated what kind of difficulty she was in, so the mystery had heightened Darby's sense of urgency. Dolly could be excitable at times and create crises that were unwarranted ... but he loved her dearly. Maybe this time she really was in danger, so he needed to get to her as soon as soon as possible.

However, thanks to the drunken fool he'd hired as a driver, Darby was now trapped and completely helpless in an overturned stagecoach on a muddy and probably rarely traveled road with a likely snowstorm on its way.

Before this sudden stagecoach wreck, Darby, with pencil in hand, had been attempting to edit the first chapter of his latest dime novel, SANTA FE SHOWDOWN for his editors in New York City. Then, without any warning, the drunken lout of a driver he'd foolishly hired in Santa Fe had spit tobacco into the headwind. The tobacco juice had been snatched by the capricious and swirling wind and sprayed through the window across Darby's face and manuscript. Enraged, Darby had clamped his hat down tight then stuck his head into the whipping wind and shouted at the driver, admonishing him to stop spitting tobacco and drinking so much whiskey.

"Driver, slow this coach down! You're taking the curves much too fast on this slippery snow and ice!"

"Shut the hell up down there!" the driver hollered back at the famous eastern dime novelist.

The Derby Man sputtered furiously and then dipped his head back inside. The driver was crazy and kept whipping the poor team of four horses. Now the drunken imbecile was roaring with demented laughter. For Darby Buckingham, it was incredibly frustrating because there was absolutely nothing he could physically do to make the driver slow down. Darby vowed that when his privately hired stagecoach stopped, he would beat the hell out of the driver and fire him on the spot.

Muttering with helpless anger and removing a silk handkerchief, Darby wiped the disgusting slime of tobacco from his thick mustache and face then the top page of his bespattered manuscript. He was in a murderous frame of mind not only because of the behavior of the driver, but for the cruel treatment the man was inflicting on the four struggling horses.

Surprising even himself, Darby had grown quite fond of horses since leaving New York City years earlier in order to go west in search of stories for his popular dime novels. He was not fond of riding them, but he respected equines and could not abide their mistreatment. He liked the way the beasts smelled and how their soft muzzles felt when he offered them a treat of sugar or a carrot. At their last rest stop, the fool driver had delighted in cutting up plugs of chewing tobacco and feeding them to the horses.

"Who the hell ever thought a horse would chew tobacco?" he'd laughed and crowed. "My gawd but these dumb bastards will eat most anything! Now all I gotta do is teach the four of 'em how to spit like a man!"

Darby hadn't found the spectacle the least bit amusing and had climbed back into the coach trying to curb his mounting anger.

And later, on the way down this mountainside traveling way too fast, he'd shouted, "Slow down and stop abusing your horses, dammit! You're going so fast I can't even put pencil to paper!"

"Too bad, dude!" the driver had shouted, lashing out at the struggling team and unleashing another bellow of crazy, drunken laughter.

Darby had given up trying to write anything

under those impossible circumstances. He'd tried in vain to brace his body to keep from being tossed about in the stagecoach. A good decade past his prime, Darby was only 5'9" tall, but he weighed nearly 250 pounds and most of it was muscle. Back in his day he had been a bare-knuckle champion fighter and a circus strongman, and he had never stopped lifting weights to maintain his enormous strength. He wore an expensive black derby hat and a frock coat often with a small flower carefully tucked through the slit in his lapel.

Although modest, Darby Buckingham was a very wealthy and famous man, but on the western frontier most who first saw him smirked or laughed outright at his citified appearance. Quite often, they had learned that to mock the Derby Man was to make a very serious mistake punishable by a sound thrashing.

Darby recalled how he'd stuck his head out of the coach once more taking a quick look at the dangers ahead and risking another spray of disgusting tobacco. "You fool, can't you see that there's a sharp bend in the road up ahead and we're going way too fast!"

"I drove this gawdamn road dozens of times! Close the window and shut the hell up!"

"You fool, I paid you to get me to Prescott in one piece. Alive! You understand me!"

"Hell yes, but you paid me in full already, so I don't much care what you want, dude!"

Darby had ducked back inside before suddenly feeling the stagecoach lurch sideways on two wheels then it crashed over and slid to a shuddering stop in the mud and blowing snow. Darby heard the horses screaming and then everything went dark as he temporarily lost consciousness.

Less than a mile away now, the three fugitives from Tennessee stared down at the wreckage.

"That stagecoach has flipped part ways over with its team of horses and they're now tangled helplessly in their harness."

"We've got to see if we can save them!" Dixie cried. "I'll stay with the mares, you and Houston race on ahead!"

The tall Ballou brothers put their heels to High Man and High Fire leaving Dixie with the exhausted and pregnant mares.

Ruff was riding the younger stallion and reached the overturned coach first. Two of the stagecoach horses were nearly dead and two were weakly thrashing in the freezing mud and slush. Just off a few dozen feet lay the twisted and broken body of the driver with a whip still clenched in his lifeless fist. From the unnatural cant of his head, Ruff knew the driver had broken his neck and died instantly.

Houston yelled to his younger brother. "I'll check if anyone is still alive inside the stagecoach. You see to the horses!"

Ruff tied High Man to a wagon wheel and yanked out his Bowie knife. He didn't have time to waste if he wanted to save the injured horses, so he slashed away their harness and managed to get the animals to their feet. One of the poor horses was clearly dying and Ruff pulled his gun and put a merciful bullet through its brain.

"Ruff! There's a big fella inside and he's alive!" Houston shouted.

Ruff spun around to face his brother. "Drag him out through the door, Houston!"

A few moments passed before Houston shouted in frustration, "Dammit, Ruff, I need your help! He's really wide and heavy."

Houston was strong, but with his injured leg he was struggling to drag the victim out of the wreckage.

"Let's each both grab one of his arms and pull like hell," Houston told his brother as a hard gust of wind sent fresh snow flying. "I can't see well enough to know how badly this poor fella is hurt."

Ruff reached in and grabbed the passenger's extended arm. Houston had been right ... the man inside was unusually heavy but when both he and Houston began pulling with all their combined strength, the body inside inched out grudgingly through the door.

"He's wearing a derby and a suit coat," Houston gritted between clenched teeth. "He's an eastern dude!"

When Darby Buckingham was laid down on the cold, muddy road, Houston and Ruff took only a moment to catch their breath. The snow was beginning to fall heavily, and the wind was picking up. About a half mile back Ruff glanced at his sister and saw her trying to force their Thoroughbreds forward at a faster pace. Ruff knew that Dixie would be anxious to reach the overturned stagecoach. His kid sister was the best of them at doctoring both horses and men.

Ruff said, "His breathing seems regular. Pulse is strong. I expect the dude will live."

Dixie finally arrived. She dismounted and hurried over to the passenger. "Is he bleeding?"

"Yeah," Houston said tightly. "He's bleeding from somewhere."

Dixie didn't wait to ask Houston to look. She had nursed many horses and soldiers back at their Wildwood Farm during the Civil War and she could suture and bandage wounds better than most doctors. She unbuttoned the easterner's black frock coat noting the fineness of the fabric. She shoved his gold pocket watch back into his vest pocket and unbuttoned his shirt, then asked Houston to help roll the man over so she could inspect the easterner's back to see if there were any critical wounds or spinal injuries.

"He's got a nasty cut on the back of his head," Dixie pronounced. "And no doubt he's got a serious concussion." She surveyed the unconscious man. "He's not tall, but he's really big!"

"Big or small," Houston said, "they die just as easy."

"I don't think he's going to die," Dixie told her brother. "Not unless it's of shock due to the head injury. But we've got to find him shelter."

Houston considered their lonesome and completely exposed surroundings. "Any suggestions?

"The stagecoach," she replied without hesitation. "It isn't tipped completely over on its side and appears to be held up partially by the dirty snow bank next to the roadway. If we can get the coach righted and seeing as how no wheels are broken, we might be able to find shelter tonight."

"Those horses are cut and in rough shape, Ruff said, sounding doubtful about the plan. "They look so banged up that they all might up and die in harness trying to pull this stagecoach the rest of the way to Prescott."

"We have to try and right this coach," Dixie said resolutely. "Once erect, it'll help that it's on a steep downgrade."

"What about the driver's body?" Ruff asked.

"If it was up to me, I'd say we leave him because it's obvious this whole mess is his stupid fault," Houston snapped in anger.

"We can't do that," Dixie objected.

"You can smell the whiskey on him from way over here," Ruff hissed with contempt. "The fool was dead drunk."

"Then no loss to the world," Houston growled. "I have little use for a man who would do this to a team of horses and a helpless passenger."

"Amen," Ruff agreed. "And I agree that we should try to right this stagecoach and get it on down the road to flat land ... but I'm not sure we have enough muscle to do the job."

Dixie studied the big coach. "We've got to think of a way. Our father would have figured out something. This passenger's life might depend on it."

Ruff studied the wreck for a moment then unfurled his rope. "With you and Houston pushing from the upside and me pulling from the downside we ought to be able to get the job done in a hurry."

"Time is wasting," Dixie told her brothers, "so let's get to it!"

Suddenly, the Derby Man groaned and then sat up taking his head in his hands. "I've taken quite a knock," he said, glancing around in confusion.

"What..."

Darby's eyes fell upon the dead driver lying in the snow. "That idiot was going much too fast because he was very drunk."

"Well," Houston said, "he paid the ultimate price for his mistake and got his fool neck broken. Mister, you've taken a bad tumble and we need to get you to shelter."

Darby Buckingham pushed himself to his knees despite the Ballou brothers trying to keep him down for a few more minutes. "I've taken harder knocks in the boxing ring. I'm going to be fine."

"That may be true," Dixie argued, "but this stagecoach needs to be righted so we can get you to Prescott."

Darby Buckingham glanced over at the wreck. "Are the horses all dead?"

"Only one is," Ruff replied not bothering to hide his anger. "Mister, you should lie back down for just a few minutes. You've got a nasty cut on the back of your head."

Darby just stared at the tall young man for a moment before asking, "Why would I lie back down in that miserable, freezing mud?"

No one had a good answer.

"Help me to my feet," Darby said extending his arms. "I heard you say that we need to right the coach. If we do that, can the surviving horses pull it down off this mountainside and on to Prescott?"

"I believe they can," Ruff told him. "But ..."

Darby didn't want to hear any more and his head was throbbing and hurt like hell. He glanced down at his ruined suit then at his expensive derby hat. "Let's all push from the topside and right this stagecoach."

"Ready!" Houston called.

"We lift on my count of three," Darby ordered.

"Mister, you're seriously hurt. Why don't you let us see if we can do it on our own first," Ruff offered.

Darby was slapping mud off himself, but now he paused with a slightly amused smile. "Very well. Give it your best!"

So, Dixie, Ruff and Houston planted their feet in the mud and heaved with all their might, but the coach remained tilted on its side.

Darby Buckingham shook his head and joined the three to press his hands to the coach. "Alright," he growled, "let's get this thing upright!"

Ruff couldn't believe how easily the heavy coach seemed to pop up from the muddy road with the big man's help before it dropped down on all four wheels.

The Ballou brothers stared at the Derby Man, knowing full well that the easterner had done the heaviest lifting.

"Don't just stand there," Darby said quietly, as he fished for a Cuban cigar in his coat pocket.

He inspected it closely, bit off the tip and found a match. He lit the cigar and while the Ballou family watched, he yanked open the stagecoach's door and painfully climbed inside.

"Miss," he said, "perhaps you would care to join me while your friends hitch the team back up and we get underway."

"They're not my friends," Dixie told the man. "They're my brothers and we're all from Tennessee. I'll get back on horseback and keep our band of Thoroughbred mares moving along closely behind the coach."

Darby closed the door and leaned back against the seat cushion. His head was pounding, and he felt beat up but fortunate to be alive as he started to collect and sort out his precious manuscript papers. Fortunately, the pages were numbered so that would quickly be taken care of to his satisfaction. Darby peered out his broken side window to study the body of the driver lying in the freezing mud. His beard was smeared with blood and tobacco and the man's eyes were wide open and staring up at a gun-metal gray and threatening sky. The driver looked as if he were smiling at his own death.

"Damn," Darby muttered, climbing back outside and nearly falling. "We can't just leave the body out here to feed scavenging animals."

Dixie said. "Then would you mind if..."

Darby knew what she was going to ask, and he'd have none of it. "That fool is not riding inside with me!"

"But..."

"We can tie his body on top of the coach," Darby said, cutting off her next words.

With a sigh of both resignation and supreme annoyance, Darby Buckingham slogged through the mud to grab the driver by his collar and drag him over to the coach. The driver wasn't all that heavy and with a mighty grunt, Darby heaved the dead man up onto the top of the coach.

The Ballou people gaped with astonishment.

Darby slapped his hands with disgust then he growled around his cigar, "He doesn't deserve a burial, but once we find a cemetery, we'll just dump him next to it and keep on moving."

"That sounds about right to me," Houston said.

"Me too," Dixie agreed.

"He might have a next of kin in Prescott," Ruff offered.

Darby scowled. "Alright," he said finally. "We'll haul him to Fort Whipple and let the Army deal with the burial."

Dixie and her brothers nodded in full agreement.

"Well," Darby said, painfully climbing back into the coach, "we can't just stand around as this storm intensifies. And I have a hell of a headache and what I need is a drink. Anyone have any Irish or Kentucky whiskey?"

"If we did, we'd be drinkin' it," Houston said. "I sure could use a couple shots of even bad whiskey right about now."

Ruff walked over and retrieved the driver's bottle. It still held a few ounces. He offered it to Darby Buckingham, but the dime novelist shook his head and decisively and slammed the door.

As the stagecoach jerked into motion Darby

Buckingham surveyed the interior of the coach. He was disgusted by the mess and carefully gathered up the pages of his manuscript then used a handkerchief to wipe mud off his coat and trousers. His shoes were ruined, and his mood was beyond foul until he glanced out the side window at the Tennessee horsemen.

The tall one named Ruff had tied his stallion to the back of the coach and climbed up to drive. The girl named Dixie was pretty and had a serious expression that told Darby she was a very responsible and sensible girl. The last one with the lame leg was devilishly handsome and he radiated an aura of danger. He would be the oldest and despite the injured leg, there was just something about the way he moved and spoke that hinted he had seen some very hard times and had probably killed men both on and off the battlefield.

Interesting family, Darby thought as he settled for an uncomfortable ride for however long as it took to find shelter from this intensifying snowstorm. The Derby Man was naturally an impatient man, and with Dolly Beavers plea for help echoing in his mind, he was never more so than on this miserable day.

CHAPTER 5

The snowstorm had hit them hard after they got underway with Darby Buckingham riding inside the coach and the dead driver roped to the roof. One of the three injured team horses quit a short time after they'd started rolling. It just stopped in a shroud of blowing snow, flayed out its shaking legs and lowered its head in a posture of abject misery.

"That poor animal is finished and needs to be unharnessed," Dixie said. "We'll have to turn around following the wagon tracks we've just made."

"I'm not sure if the last two horses can pull the stage."

"Me neither," Dixie admitted.

Ruff cut the horse free. "Sure hate to leave him out here by himself. But maybe he'll just follow along with our mares."

"Ash Fork was a decent sized town," Houston offered. "Had two or three saloons, a big mercantile, law office, hotel and a stable barn … even a church and a gun shop. I agree that we should turn back.

We won't make it to without resting our mares and taking shelter for the night."

Darby stuck his head out of the window while carefully hanging on to the brim of his derby to keep it from sailing off in the gusting wind. His head was spinning and for the first time he realized he had double vision from the concussion he'd sustained in the wreck. He also felt sick to his stomach. Having been in many brutal bare knuckles' fights in his younger days, he was well aware that serious head blows often manifested their damage a short time after they occurred. Apparently, that was what was happening to him now.

"Why," he gasped, "are we stopping out here in the middle of nowhere in a blizzard?"

When the situation was explained to him, Darby weakly nodded in agreement. "I want to get to Prescott, but not if it means risking the lives of the horses. And I need to lie down and get some rest. So, turn his stagecoach around and we'll put up tonight in Ash Fork and wait out the storm."

"It could last several days," Ruff warned. "And the road between here and Prescott might be snowed over so deep we can't get through for a while."

"Better late than dead," Darby answered, falling weakly back in his seat.

It wasn't easy to get the stagecoach turned around, but they did it despite the howling wind and blowing snow. As hoped, the spent horse now freed from harness fell in with the Ballou Thoroughbreds behind the coach. Ash Fork was only about four miles back, but they couldn't have made it any farther with the stagecoach because their tracks were already filling with snow and the wind was shrieking.

They went directly to the largest stable barn in town. There was no one in attendance so they took care of things themselves.

"I'll get the two team horses unharnessed," Ruff shouted, "then I'll help the dude out of the stagecoach and we'll bring all the other horses into the barn and out of this cold, cutting wind."

Dixie and Houston set to work and in less than five minutes, they slammed the big door of the barn shut and were suddenly enveloped in freezing darkness. Ruff had looked into the barn before the door was shut and he saw only a few stalls with horses. There was hay in the loft and not much else except harnesses and saddles lined up along a wall.

"I saw a couple of lanterns on that post!" he shouted. "Let's get some light in here and set to work!"

The last of the horsemen worked fast using empty grain sacks to rub down their exhausted and pregnant mares. Finally, they took care of High Man, High Fire and the injured stagecoach horses using horse liniments and salves they found on a shelf. By the time they finished, everyone was sweaty and steaming with body heat.

"Let's toss some hay and get ourselves over to the hotel," Ruff said. "The dude looks to be in rough shape."

When they left the barn, the empty and now deserted stagecoach was already coated with fresh snow and there were a pair of legs dangling off the roof.

"Somebody is in for a helluva shock when they see that dead driver," Houston offered, with a grim smile.

"Yeah," Ruff added. "I imagine it'll cause quite the stir."

Darby Buckingham had to be assisted out of the coach. He clutched his satchel and a thick leather binder that protected his manuscript and writing supplies.

Momentarily revived by the hard, freezing wind, he surveyed the town and swore under his breath because it was not at all a place where he would have chosen. The main street was deserted and most of the businesses were closed because of the weather.

"I know it probably isn't up to your standards," Dixie said, "but hopefully it's only for a night or two and then we can move on if that weather allows us to get to Prescott."

"It'll do," Darby said, putting a hand on the coach to steady himself for a moment. His head was pounding and his double vision was a real concern. He knew he'd taken a severe head blow when the stagecoach had crashed.

"Are you going to be alright?" Houston asked, coming to his side and easing Darby's arm across his shoulder. "We don't have far to walk to that main hotel."

"I'll be fine by tomorrow. It's just been a long and eventful trip. I'm a little beat up, wet, freezing and filthy from the mud. I need a hot bath and a good meal. A few shots of whiskey will then set me up nicely for tonight."

"I hope the hotel isn't full," Dixie fretted. "In weather like this it might be we'll have to make do in the barn or some other miserable place tonight."

"I think not," the Derby Man managed to say. "No matter the cost, I'll find us decent accommodations. But that driver tied up on the roof will freeze as hard as hickory."

"This ground being frozen, he'll probably be wrapped up by the local mortician and stay frozen awhile," Ruff said. "Suit him right for what he did to those wagon horses and to you, sir."

Despite feeling rocky, Darby's thick mustache twitched with amusement and his blue lips turned up at their corners with a slight smile. Even if he'd tried, he could not have expressed his own feelings about the body of the driver any better.

Although it could not have been more than fifty yards between the barn and the hotel, it seemed like a mile. Darby didn't like being helped physically, but he was in no condition to walk through a storm without Houston's strong and solid assistance. When they pushed into the lobby of the hotel, they all just stood dripping wet and panting from exhaustion. Darby's eyes swept across the lobby and he was pleasantly surprised. There were thick carpets, polished flagstone floors, long, handsome curtains and a beautiful registration desk behind which stood a well-groomed clerk.

"They even have dining here," Ruff said in a hushed voice, pointing to a wide doorway through which could be seen a room full of diners. "I sure could use a big, juicy beefsteak!"

"I'll have a room and a hot bath in that order," Darby said to the hotel clerk as he wobbled over to the registration book. "And I'll need someone to clean my clothing."

"He also needs a doctor," Dixie added. "He's taken quite a blow to the back of his head."

"We do have ... well, some people call him a doctor and others call him a drunken butcher. However, we are very proud and pleased to let you know that we have a Chinese family that'll do an excellent cleaning and pressing job even though your suit is quite a disaster ... if you don't mind my saying so."

Darby stiffened at the impertinence. "Not that it matters to me, but you can be sure that I'll replace it on the very day that I reach Prescott."

The clerk nodded. "And about our, uh, doctor? In truth the man is almost certainly drunk by this late hour. He's only reasonably sober before noon."

Darby understood. This town was too poor to support a well-trained physician so t they'd only have someone who acted as a doctor and tooth puller.

"Let's dispense with your pathetic doctor," Darby said, turning to the Ballou girl. "After we're settled and I've cleaned myself up, will you have another look at my scalp wound?"

"Of course."

"We only have four rooms left," the clerk told them. "They are our finest and the cost will be higher."

"Hang the cost!" Darby snapped irritably. "Just as long as the rooms are clean, and I get that hot bath and whiskey. What about your dining room that appears to be very popular?"

"We have an excellent cook and never serve spoiled meat . . . but it's beef only."

"Glad to hear it. We'll want steaks two hours from now."

"Very good." The clerk paused. "Sir, you really do look unwell. And are you by any chance one of our new and important territorial officials sent from Washington?"

"No," Darby said curtly, "and right now I'm in no mood for idle talk."

"Yes sir."

"This is Mr. Darby Buckingham," Dixie informed the hotel clerk. "He's America's most successful dime novelist. He hired a private coach, but the driver got drunk on that steep downgrade out of the mountains and overturned the coach."

The clerk glanced at the door as if he expected one more guest to arrive. "Is the driver also badly injured?"

"He's dead and lashed to the roof of the stagecoach," Houston answered. "My advice is to leave him alone until the storm breaks and then stack him up with the firewood until a thaw."

The clerk gaped. "Do you know the man's name?"

"Everett Pitt," Darby said, spitting the name out like an oath.

"My God! I know the man well. He has a reputation for getting drunk while driving a stage. He owns that big barn where you probably just stabled your horses. Keeps the stagecoach inside when he's not driving."

"Miss Ballou told me that there were a few horses already in the barn."

"Yes, in weather like this, people just put them up there and hope no one notices so they don't have to pay."

"I see. Now how about a room, a hot bath and good whiskey!"

"Of course! And what about your three southern friends?"

"How do they concern you?" Darby asked bluntly.

"Well, you are obviously a gentleman of means but I just hope they have enough money to take care of themselves," the clerk fretted. "It would not be unusual if we were snowed in for several days. It could get expensive for these younger people."

"If they run short of money, I will help them out. After all, they saved my life on that mountainside."

Darby scribbled his name in the guest book and added the address of his New York apartment. He extracted a roll of bills. "How much for one night for the lot of us ... and the steaks?"

The clerk's eyes narrowed, "Ummm ..."

It was all too obvious that his fellow was gauging the easterner for how much money he could afford so Darby grabbed the clerk's coat and pulled him up on his toes. "What is your normal rate!"

"Two dollars each," the clerk squeaked, struggling to free himself from Darby's powerful grasp. "With the baths and it even includes tomorrow's breakfast."

Darby released the clerk, slammed down the money and they were all quickly given room keys. Despite his dizziness and double vision, he made his way across the lobby yelling over his shoulder, "Start the bath water heating and bring me your best whiskey in an unopened bottle."

"Right away, Mr. Buckingham!"

The truth of the matter was that Darby Buckingham was not only injured, he was in a dark, dark mood. He didn't like the idea of being stuck in Ash Fork any longer than was necessary and was very concerned about Dolly Beavers. Had she succumbed to illness? Or perhaps someone had robbed and seriously injured her? Or maybe it was something even worse. Whatever her circumstances, he needed to reach Dolly's side because he loved her. After all, they had been through a lot together over the past few years and she had been helpful and wonderful company, always cheerful and quite resourceful.

CHAPTER 6

Darby Buckingham luxuriated in the deep-sided bathtub. A grinning Chinaman kept bringing him hot water and little pots of tea, but Darby waved the tea off and kept asking the man to bring him whiskey—or at least wine. That didn't work but eventually the hotel clerk arrived with a crystal decanter of whiskey that wasn't anything exceptional, but it did ease the pounding in Darby's head.

He was starting to doze off in the tub when he heard Dixie calling from just outside the door. "Are you decent, Mr. Buckingham?"

"No!"

"Sink down in the tub and try to be more civil in your tone of voice," Dixie ordered. "And cover yourself with a towel or wash cloth. I want to take care of that nasty head wound before I clean myself up and go to dinner."

Before Darby could formulate a reason why that was entirely a bad idea, the door opened, and Dixie entered the steamy bathroom with her medical kit.

"How are you feeling?"

"Much better," he admitted. "Don't you think this ought to wait until I'm dressed?"

"I've already been waiting nearly an hour," Dixie said, unable to hide her impatience. "I'm still dirty and hungry and I'm disappointed that there isn't a single real doctor in Ash Fork."

She pulled a chair up beside the tub and sat down behind Darby. He felt her probe his lacerated scalp. "Ouch! You're not handling a horse, young lady!"

"I'm definitely not a *lady,* sir."

She probed his scalp, feeling the deep laceration. "You have a very nasty laceration on the back of your head. I should probably put stitches in it, but then I'd need to use a horse needle and shave the back of your head."

Darby had never seen a "horse needle" but it sounded awful. "No sutures!"

"Alright," she agreed. "The bleeding has stopped, and the wound has clotted. Is your head still pounding and are you seeing double?"

"Not since I started drinking whiskey."

He almost had to chuckle to himself at the absurdity of whiskey taking away double vision.

She came around to face him. A highly embarrassed Darby sank as far down in the tub as he could and covered his privates.

"Miss, this is very unseemly."

"Mr. Buckingham, I don't a whit about being *unseemly,*" she told him. "I grew up with five older brothers and I've seen it all. When you are finally dressed, I have some of Dr. Hammer's Horse

Ointment that works wonders on lacerations. I've used successfully on men, dogs and horses and I want to ..."

The idea of having some greasy and probably foul-smelling horse ointment smeared into his hair was abhorrent. "Absolutely not."

Dixie cocked her head to one side and gave him a half smile. "You are a very, very stubborn man, Mr. Buckingham. We've already figured out that you have a lot of money from the clothes you wear and the fact that you could afford to hire your own private stagecoach. And you said you were a popular dime novelist."

"All true. And before that I was a bare-knuckle champion in New York and even earlier a circus strong man," Darby told her with a flourish of his glass of whiskey. "But I prefer to be regarded as just another humble writer in search of stories out in the West."

"And you have a story waiting in Prescott?"

"Yes, I think so and I have a deadline from my New York editors who are most anxious to publish another of my novels. When the coach tipped over, I was already on page eighty and the words were coming fast."

"I should admit that neither I nor my brothers read dime novel westerns. But now that I've made your acquaintance, I would very much like to read one of your works."

"I don't have the talent to write great literature," Darby modestly admitted. "But I am one hell of a fine storyteller."

"That's the most important thing," Dixie assured him.

"I agree. And before we part company, I'll give you a list of my personal favorite novels and even see that you get autographed copies when things get settled."

"Thank you! I'd like that very much," Dixie said. "Mind if I have a swig or two of your whiskey? It seems to have done wonders for your disposition and it's been a long, hard and cold day."

Darby frowned because she seemed too young to drink whiskey ... but then again, she had been of enormous help so he could hardly refuse. "There is a clean glass on my bed stand. Help yourself, Miss Ballou."

"Dixie," she corrected, removing the bottle from beside the bathtub and then finding the glass and pouring three fingers.

Darby watched as she downed the whiskey straight and poured two more fingers. "Thank you, that was really good and warmed me right down to my gizzard!"

Darby studied her for a moment. "You and your brothers did save my life. If you had not come along, I'd be as dead and frozen as the driver. And as a writer, I'm curious about you three. Do you mind telling me why you are out here in the Arizona Territory with those magnificent horses?"

"I'll give you the short version. We had to leave our plantation and horse ranch because of the war. We had given the Confederate Army all but the last few horses you see now. My father refused to give them the last of a bloodline that he'd spent his entire life developing. His refusal resulted in a gun battle with a foolish captain and both he and my father were killed. We were then branded as traitors and to this very day there are vengeful people who still want us dead. In fact, they even put a bounty on our heads and so we've been running ever since."

Darby listened quietly. Finally, when it seemed Dixie was finished, he asked, "How long will you keep running?"

"Good question and one we'd love to know the answer to." Dixie shrugged. "Maybe we've run far enough, and Prescott is where we make our stand. If people come to kill us or take our Thoroughbreds ... we will fight them to the death."

"May I ask you just one more question before you go?"

"Sure, provided it isn't too personal."

"All three of you have dark complexions and I detect Indian facial features."

"Our mother was a full-blooded Cherokee so we're half-breeds." Dixie took a sip of her whiskey and smacked her lips. "Does that bother you, sir?"

"No, it intrigues me. Go on."

"Our Cherokee mother's name was Lucinda Eldee Starr and her Indian name was *Ah-na-hi Noxie.*"

"I take it she is dead."

"Yes, she died six years before the Civil War helping her Cherokee people during a terrible cholera epidemic that swept through the Great Smoky Mountains of North Carolina. Most of the Cherokee and other Indian peoples who survived the cholera were rounded up and driven by the United

States Army and marched to Oklahoma in what will be forever remembered as the *Trail of Tears.*"

Dixie tried to say more but she was too choked up with emotion, so she covered her eyes, then looked away fighting back tears.

Darby poured a little more whiskey in both their glasses. "I've heard about that historic atrocity and it was shameful of President Andrew Jackson. He was the very officer who had used the Indians to win the Battle of New Orleans even though he was greatly outnumbered against the British. What a foul betrayal to your people!"

"Yes," Dixie agreed. "And when the roundup of The People began, quite a few of Mother's tribe hid in the forests and were never caught and relocated to Oklahoma. They still live in small villages up in the most remote parts of the mountains."

"Did you ever visit them?" Darby asked.

"A few times ... but when we did, we knew that we were putting them at risk, so our visits were very rare and secretive." Dixie took a deep breath. "Do you mind if I finish up here and go take a bath? What I need besides your whiskey is a good meal and a soft bed."

"I understand. After a while I will meet you all in the dining room and buy you a fine meal."

"You're very generous."

There was a long silence and then Dixie quietly, "We are not traitors of the South. But there is little doubt that, had we remained in Tennessee, we would have been hanged or bushwhacked."

"I can very well understand that."

Darby was moved not only by this pretty young woman's story, but also by the obvious depth of her pain. "My dear," he said quietly, "have you changed your family name?'

"That wasn't even considered. You see, our horses, especially the two stallions, will always give our true identities away. We are the Ballou family and we are, above all … horsemen."

"You're a horse *woman,*" Darby corrected.

"No," Dixie countered. "I'm not. But we shouldn't waste our time splitting the meaning of words. We look forward to sharing dinner with you tonight."

"Well said," Darby replied, realizing that this difficult conversation was over. "In that case, and before you go, would you please toss me that towel and return what's left of my whiskey?"

"With pleasure," Dixie answered and then she was gone.

Their dinner was surprisingly good … tender steaks, bean sprouts, sourdough bread and apple pie for dessert along with two bottles of respectable French wine.

"Mr. Buckingham, how many dime novels have you written?" Dixie asked.

"Twenty-three. The earlier ones were not up to my standards, so I marched into my publisher's office and demanded that I either be allowed to go to the West and write about events and people I would meet, or I would quit writing altogether."

"Your publisher must have agreed," Houston said.

"Yes, he did. There was too much money to be

lost if I quit writing, so they gave me free rein and a generous expense account. And I've had quite the adventures doing my research for stories," Darby said with a smile. "And I met a fine woman that has become very dear to me. However, right now she is in Prescott and I fear she is in great difficulty or danger. That's why I'm so anxious to be on my way tomorrow."

"What is she like?" Dixie asked.

Darby considered the question carefully before answering. "I find it hard to describe Miss Dolly Beavers. She is ... well, very fun loving and adventurous. And perhaps most importantly she thinks I am the greatest American writer of all time ... but of course I am not."

"But if she thinks so," Dixie said, grinning, "that's important. Right?"

"Yes," Darby sheepishly admitted. "I have to admit that's true."

"Then let's toast to Miss Dolly Beavers and to love," Houston said, raising his glass.

Darby nodded with approval and stifled a yawn. He was beginning to really like these three young Tennessee horsemen.

"Can you tell us a little more about yourself?" Dixie asked.

"Well, to begin with, I grew up in a wealthy family who wanted me to be either an attorney or a doctor. But I was restless and went to Europe, then bounced around for a few years doing this and that," Darby explained. "Both my parents died in a train wreck and being the only child, I inherited quite a bit of money, a house and some expensive furniture that I really had never cared for. I sold everything and moved into Manhattan and met some interesting people. Artists, serious writers, sculptors, poets ... that sort. I tried to be a literary writer but found worrying about every word was tedious to the extreme. Same with poetry. I even took a few art classes and embarrassed myself.

"One night with nothing to do, I went to the circus. And afterward, when I was heading back to my apartment, I witnessed an attack on the circus strong man. He was an amazing physical specimen and not only incredibly strong, but he also had learned the art of fisticuffs. He easily whipped his four attackers and went on his way as if nothing much had happened."

Dixie smiled. "And you followed him?"

"How did you guess?" Darby asked. "I offered to buy him dinner and drinks and by the time the circus was ready to leave town the next week, we were good friends. He offered to help me become very, very strong by applying myself to a rigorous lifting and training program that he had religiously followed for many years. He pushed me extremely hard in the correct way to lift enormously heavy weights. I had no regrets about leaving New York."

"It seems odd that a rich young man would do such a thing," Houston commented.

"It *was* odd, and it probably saved me from wasting my life endlessly seeking pleasures and new places," Darby admitted. "For the next eighteen months we traveled back and forth across this country doing all the big cities. Then we toured Europe. All that time I was lifting heavier and heavier weights. Meanwhile, my circus friend ruined his back attempting a lift of four hundred pounds and I was able to take his place."

"Four hundred pounds?" Houston asked, almost in disbelief.

"Yes. But understand that heavy lifting is almost as much about technique as it is pure power."

"What happened to him after his back injury?" Ruff asked.

"We stayed friends and for a few months he attempted to travel with the circus but sitting on a train or stagecoach for long periods was excruciating and he had to retire. He now lives in my large apartment in New York and takes care of a destructive but amusing tomcat that I am ridiculously fond of. He does odd jobs when he is able, and I pay him a salary to watch over my apartment which has some very expensive paintings that I've collected. The arrangement works well for us both."

"How long did you travel as a circus strongman?" Dixie asked.

Darby considered the question for a few moments. "Almost three years."

"And you were a bare-knuckles fighter?" Houston asked.

"A champion, although that fact is disputed by some. I fought the best, both in America and Europe.'"

"Your face doesn't show too much damage," Dixie said.

"I focused on defensive skills and I had a knock-out punch so most of my matches were short."

"Why did you quit the ring?"

Darby drummed his fingers on the table with an expression of great sadness. "I almost killed a man in Baltimore one night. After that, I just couldn't fight in the ring anymore and I was ready for another challenge. By chance, when traveling, I found a couple of discarded dime novels, read them and found them fascinating and preposterous. I thought I could do better."

"So, you became far more famous as a writer than a circus strongman or champion fighter?"

Darby lit a Cuban cigar and blew a smoke ring over their heads. "Yes, and the money was much better with less pain."

"So, you came west and started researching and writing truer stories," Ruff said.

"Exactly."

All three of the Ballou horsemen leaned forward with the same question, but Darby foresaw it and smiled. "No, I never speak of my story while it is in the creative progress. But someday, you can read the novel."

Darby raised his glass. "To us and to our friendship. You have my heartfelt thanks for your assistance and I'll forever be in your debt."

"As you know, we are also on our way to Prescott," Dixie said, "We'd like to travel with you."

"It would be my pleasure to share your company," Darby replied. "So long as we can be on our way as early as possible."

"As soon as the snow stops flying. We can give

you a horse to ride and ..."

"I really try to avoid riding horses," Darby said bluntly. "But I'm not about to climb back in that stagecoach, so I'll rent or buy a buggy and accompany you fine young people."

"Then that's what we'll do," Dixie said with her brothers nodding in agreement. "We'll all go together to Prescott and see what opportunities Arizona's new territorial capital holds."

"And, if you've no objections, we'd be honored to meet Miss Dolly Beavers," Houston added.

"Yes," Darby said quietly. "And help me deal with whatever trouble she might be in."

CHAPTER 7

The next morning Darby awoke with the sun shining through his hotel room curtains. He gingerly touched the back of his scalp and was relieved that there had been no bleeding during the night. Even better, he stood up and there was no dizziness or blurred vision. It looked like he was going to be able to make it down to Prescott today. First thing he would do after his arrival in the territorial capital would be to buy new clothes. Even though the Chinese laundryman had worked hard, his expensive suit and shirt were still faintly stained by mud and blood.

If my dear Dolly is alright, everything will be fine, Darby told himself as he hurriedly finished dressing and went to the dining room where he was expecting his young Tennessee friends to be waiting for him and their breakfast.

But the Ballou horsemen were not in the dining room and it was strangely quiet in contrast to the evening before when it had been filled with noisy and boisterous customers.

Darby was famished so he ordered his breakfast and coffee. He was halfway through his meal when Dixie burst through the door, spotted Darby and rushed over to his table.

"Something terrible happened last night," she began. "Someone stole five of our Thoroughbreds!"

Darby was so shocked he almost spilled his coffee. "Does this town have a sheriff?"

"Yes. My brothers are looking for him right now. He and his deputy should be here soon."

Almost immediately, Ruff and Houston barged into the dining room.

Darby saw the anger and consternation on their handsome faces and said, "Dixie tells me that five of your valuable horses were stolen last night. Were the stallions among them?"

"No," Houston said tightly. "I'm sure they tried to steal High Man and High Fire, but the stallions were too difficult to handle by strangers. We cannot afford to lose those mares, Mr. Buckingham. My brother and I are going after the thieves as soon as we can gather provisions."

"If the sheriff ever arrives, he'll probably want to go with you."

"We don't need him."

Darby shrugged. "The tracks should be easy to follow given the snow. Any idea how many horse thieves you're after?"

Ruff shook his head. "When we arrived last evening in that blizzard, I'm pretty sure there were four horses in the barn and now there are none, and the bridles and saddles are gone. I don't think there's any question that whoever owned the horses went to the barn last night and saw the chance to steal our valuable animals. The tracks are all messed up in the barn and outside as well as there have been a number of riders and a couple of wagons that have gone down the street early this morning."

"I would help you," Darby said, "but given my poor horsemanship, I'd only slow you down."

"That's right," Houston agreed. "Would you help Dixie watch over the mares we have left and make sure she comes to no harm? If you'd do that much, it would greatly ease our minds."

"Of course!"

"Dixie will insist on bedding down in the stable tonight to make sure that we don't lose the rest of the Thoroughbreds," Ruff explained. "She is a good shot if anyone comes to try and steal the last few mares."

Darby wiped biscuit crumbs from his thick black mustache. "Do you think that is possible?"

"I spoke to several people early this morning after we found our horses were missing and they said that the mines in these parts are playing out and there are a lot of desperate men willing to do most anything to survive. So, to answer your question, yes, it's very possible that more thieves would come while Houston and I are gone hunting for horse thieves."

"I understand."

"Mr. Buckingham, no offense meant, but have you ever even fired a gun?" Houston asked bluntly.

"Of course! I carry a derringer and I am very

adept with a shotgun, although I'm not at all accurate with a pistol."

"If other thieves come again you won't need to be accurate, but you will need to stand your ground and protect our sister and the few mares that weren't stolen."

"I'll do that and whatever else is required, and not waver in the face of death or danger," Darby said solemnly. "On that you have my word."

"That's exactly what we needed to hear."

"Would you like to have a bite of breakfast?" Darby asked. "Most likely you're going to miss some meals."

The brothers exchanged quick glances before Ruff said, "We'll go get ready and stop back by for a hurried breakfast before we take up the chase. Our mares are heavy with foal and they won't be able to move fast. I don't know how much of a head start the horse thieves have on us, but it can't be more than six hours. Mounted on our stallions, we'll make up the time fast."

Homer Gentry, Ash Fork's mayor and editor of the small, weekly newspaper, hurried inside the hotel and caught Dixie in the lobby. "Miss, I understand you lost some Thoroughbreds from Everett Pitts' barn last night."

"That's right. My brothers are readying themselves to give chase."

"What about waiting for Sheriff Wade Holt and his cousin, Cletus, who's a part-time deputy?"

"If they can get ready to ride quickly, they're welcome to come." Dixie's eyes narrowed, "But

Mayor, if necessary, my brothers will take up the chase without your sheriff and his deputy."

"I'm sure your brothers are very capable, but they might be taking on more than they can handle. From what I can gather, it sounds like the horse thieves knew what they were doing."

"They did," Dixie agreed. "But Ruff and Houston are crack shots and they can handle whatever they might face."

"I certainly hope so," the editor said, looking doubtful. "This town is full of thieves, drunks and killers."

"Then why on earth are you here?"

"Good question and one I often ask myself," Homer admitted. "The answer is that my wife and I stay because we own a huge printing press and our newspaper building and I'm too old to start over somewhere new. On top of that, I believe that this town has a bright ranching and farming future despite the mines failing. We know that the Atlantic & Pacific Railroad is coming through here and when that happens, it will be a boom town. There is even talk that this might be a major repair and switching location for the trains."

"Now I understand why there is so much activity here."

"Yes, and we have a high-water table so that's never going to limit our growth." The editor frowned. "But there is something else I wanted to see you about and I hope you don't mind my bringing up the subject given the suddenly desperate situation you and your brothers find yourselves in this morning."

"I'm in a hurry so please state your mind directly."

"I want to interview you along with that easterner who wears a derby hat. I'll write a story that will sell a lot of newspapers this week. My circulation is down, and it would be a tremendous boost."

"You can interview me," Dixie said. "But I can't speak for Mr. Buckingham, who may refuse."

The editor's eyes lit up with excitement. "Are you referring to Darby Buckingham, the famous dime novelist?"

"Why yes, is he *that* well known?"

"Darby Buckingham is the leading dime novelist of these times. I've read several of his books and although they are quite fantastic, they are a *wonderful* read. He is a gifted storyteller with a sly and deliciously dry sense of humor. My very favorite of his dime novels is titled *Twenty Guns to Texas.* If you haven't yet read it, you really should."

"I'll try to remember that. Now, if you'll excuse me?"

"Of course! But please don't forget to ask Mr. Buckingham about an interview."

"Alright," Dixie promised. "But what is taking Sheriff Holt so long to get here?"

"I'm sure he'll show up soon with his deputy. Your brothers really should wait for their help before they go after those horse thieves."

"They can't afford to waste time waiting around for your local lawmen," Dixie said, not bothering to hide her irritation.

The editor nodded with understanding.

Ruff and Houston were ready to gulp down a quick breakfast and ride. They'd each brought extra ammunition, tins of canned meat and heavy bedrolls in case they were forced to sleep outdoors in the freezing cold. They'd be traveling fast and hoped to overtake the horse thieves by sundown. Horse thieving being a hanging offense, they expected that however many men they were hunting would fight to the death. They had one purpose in mind and that was to retrieve their stolen mares come hell or high water.

"You must be the Ballou brothers," a loud voice called from the lobby as a tall, rugged man with a badge marched into the hotel dining room. He was followed closely by his deputy, Cletus, a slovenly man with a full beard and the dirtiest clothes Darby had ever seen on a human being. His close-set eyes were bloodshot, and his hair was matted with dirt.

Darby Buckingham was a very good judge of character. The sheriff was probably no more than thirty-five years old and he looked tough and confident despite deep lines of fatigue on his mud-splattered face. Cletus looked like he'd been dragged out of a pig sty.

"We had our mares stolen last night," Houston snapped. "And you would be Sheriff Wade Holt and that fella would be your cousin and deputy, Cletus. Nice of you men to finally show up this morning."

Holt's dark eyes momentarily flashed with anger, but then he took a deep breath and pulled up a chair to join them while his deputy stared at the leftover breakfast at the table.

"Johnny Rebs," Holt began, "me and my deputy were up late last night and just learned your precious mares were stolen out of Everett Pitts' barn, which you had no permission to use."

"Well," Houston said quietly, "you might not have taken the time to notice, but Pitts isn't talking or taking money anymore."

"Oh, and why is that?"

"Because the sonofabitch is frozen solid on the roof of his stagecoach and probably blanketed with a couple feet of snow."

The deputy's jaw dropped. "Old Everett is dead? Who killed him?"

"He killed himself when he overturned the stagecoach I'd hired coming down the damned mountainside to your town," Darby said.

"And who the hell are you?"

"I'm a friend of the Ballou family and I can't imagine why you're asking dumb questions instead of taking up the hunt along with Ruff and Houston Ballou."

The sheriff face flushed with anger. "We can talk later, *dude*."

"I won't have the pleasure of staying in Ash Fork long, so you had better find the horse thieves and get back soon."

Sheriff Holt gave Darby a hard look then turned to Houston and Ruff. "Look," he said, throwing up both hands and offering a tolerant smile, "me and my deputy know this country very well so give us an hour or two to eat and saddle fresh horses and we'll all take up the trail."

"Sorry," Houston said bluntly, "but our mares are out there being driven hard and we mean to get them back by tonight. That means we aren't waiting for you or anyone else. If the snow starts flying heavy again, tracks could be snowed over and lost."

"I'm sorry to hear you say that," the sheriff told him, "because it means I'm going to have to arrest you for interfering with the law. Me and Cletus are the ones that are paid to catch and arrest horse thieves and other outlaws."

Dixie saw her brothers stiffen and knew they were about to explode, so she said, "Sheriff, how does taking up the trail in two hours sound? We don't figure the thieves can be that far away from Ash Fork."

"What makes you say that? My understanding is that they stole your horses sometime last night."

"Our Thoroughbred mares are all pregnant," Ruff explained. "They won't be able to run, or even move fast walking, through fresh snow. And they're too valuable to leave behind."

"That makes sense. Alright, give us two hours and my deputy and I will be ready. With four of us, we stand a better chance in a gunfight."

"Houston," Dixie said, "for the sake of our horses and yourselves, you need to accept the sheriff's offer. Ruff, you as well. I've lost enough family already these past years."

Ruff reluctantly nodded then Houston did the same. "Okay, two hours and then we're riding."

"Cletus and I will be mounted on fresh horses and waiting in front of the hotel," Holt promised, consulting his pocket watch. "And don't you southern boys leave early or a whole new war is going to start between us."

"Is that a threat?" Houston asked quietly.

"A promise. I'm sure you are tough, but you don't look like professional gunmen. Me and Deputy Burr are professionals. Just keep that in mind."

Dixie studied her brothers. What Sheriff Holt didn't understand was that both Ruff and Houston were very fast and dead shots.

"All right, Sheriff," Houston managed to growl.

"Then it's settled," Darby told everyone. "Dixie and I will take care of things here, expecting you to return with the mares in a day or two at most."

"We'll talk to you later, dude," Cletus hissed, spitting tobacco juice on the floor near Darby's shoe.

"I can't wait," Darby replied with a cold smile.

Cletus hadn't expected that answer from the easterner and he tried to think of a smart retort to show he was not afraid of anyone, but instead grabbed a slice of toast from the table, stuffed into his mouth before leaving the dining room.

The sheriff studied Darby Buckingham. "You would be wise not to goad my cousin, sir. He may look the slovenly fool, but he is fearless in a fight and very good with a gun."

"I'll try hard to remember that. Now, don't you think you should go get ready for the manhunt?"

The sheriff snorted with derision and left the room.

"Not much of a pair to ride with, are they?" Houston said. "I wish we'd have left before they arrived."

"You might be right about that," Ruff agreed. "But we've reached an agreement with the sheriff and we'll hold to it."

"Sit down and have a good breakfast," Darby suggested. "The ham and eggs aren't bad, and the sourdough biscuits are rather exceptional."

"I'm hungry and I could use some hot coffee," Ruff said.

"Me too," Houston agreed.

"Then let's eat and get better acquainted," Darby told them. "Have you ever read one of my dime novels?"

Both men shook their heads. Darby shrugged as if it did not matter. "Well, when the dust settles a bit and we've gotten settled in Prescott, I'll give all three of you a different novel to read and enjoy."

"You carry your own dime novels in your bags?" Dixie asked.

"Of course. Giving people something entertaining to read gives me real pleasure." Darby paused, looking at each of them. "No offense intended, but you can all read, can't you?"

"Sure," Dixie replied. "We can even read a little Cherokee."

Houston winked. "And we can even count to twenty on our fingers and toes."

It took a split second for Darby to realize the man had made a joke and he barked a laugh. "In that case I promise never again to underestimate you."

CHAPTER 8

Two hours later the sheriff and his deputy were mounted on fresh horses in front of the hotel ready to take up the chase. It took them less than ten minutes to pick up the tracks of the Thoroughbred mares and the men who'd taken them out of Pitts' barn sometime the previous night. And although it was impossible to tell for certain, it looked like there were four or possibly five horse thieves.

Sheriff Holt said, "They're heading up toward Saw Tooth Peak and Rocky Gorge."

"We'll find them," Ruff promised. "I just hope they haven't injured any of our mares."

Houston looked sideways at him and shouted, "Whoever they are, they're going to knock on hell's gates this day."

Sheriff Holt overheard that remark and wasn't pleased. "Remember, I'm the law and the one in charge and if I go down, Cletus will be in charge. If you Tennessee boys think you're just going to open fire on these people, you better get something straight. I'll demand their surrender. If they refuse, then we'll do what's necessary."

"Why would they ever agree to surrender given they're going to get hanged?" Houston demanded.

Cletus spoke for the first time. "They might know some people on a jury and get off."

Ruff couldn't hide his surprise because what the deputy had said made sense. "Why would there be a trial? This is a clear case of horse thieving which is a hanging offense."

The deputy had the eyes of a reptile … cold and black. He hadn't spoken hardly a word so far and now he spat a stream of tobacco and squinted at Ruff, then drew a sleeve across his runny nose. "Them boys we're followin' might be kinfolk that me and the sheriff can talk sense to. No use in killin' 'em if they give up the horses peaceable like."

Houston's handsome face darkened. "Dammit, I've never heard of such a thing as letting that kind of men go without prison or a noose."

"I'm just sayin' you can't never tell what will happen. That's all I'm sayin', Johnny Reb."

Ruff and his brother looked to Sheriff Holt who just shrugged his shoulders. "Cletus just has a different way of lookin' at things and sometimes his way actually makes good sense."

Houston was so angry he prodded his horse on ahead and Ruff followed close behind with a worried expression.

By mid-afternoon the storm had passed, but the temperature had dropped and the wind was blasting off the mountains. The four of them had been pushing hard on the trail but it was clear that the men they were chasing were also traveling as fast as the pregnant Ballou mares allowed.

"I'm especially worried about the mares farthest along to their time to foal," Ruff fretted to his brother. "They ought to be resting in a nice barn with plenty of feed and out of this hard wind. This is bad, Houston."

"You're better'n I am at reading tracks and sign. How far do you think they are in front of us?"

"We'll overtake 'em in a couple more hours."

"Then we ought to be able to do it before dark," Houston said, tugging down the brim of his hat.

Ruff took a deep breath and let it out slow to try and release some of the tension he was feeling inside. Judging from the tracks it still looked like there were four horse thieves ... perhaps five. Growing up in Tennessee, it had been every boy's job to learn how to fish, track and hunt—deer and occasionally a bear, but more often ducks, squirrels and even ground hogs, if there was nothing else that would put meat on the table.

As for the sheriff and his deputy, there was no telling how they were going to handle the situation. Sheriff Holt had the look of a man who could be counted on in a gunfight ... but his deputy seemed wild and unpredictable and would bear close watching.

"If this bunch sees us rushing 'em up behind, maybe they'll dismount and use our mares as shields knowing we'd be damned reluctant to open fire and risk killing them," Houston reasoned. "That's what I'd do, if I were them."

"Me too," Ruff admitted.

"We should have a plan of some sort."

"When you come up with one be sure and let me know."

A few minutes later, they spotted something moving toward them out of a gap in the mountains.

"It's a freight wagon," Ruff said, "with a team of six mules."

"I'll handle this!" Sheriff Holt yelled galloping hard up the road with his deputy in close pursuit.

The driver hauled his team to a stop and lifted his hands. "I ain't got no more money or anything of value! Some men already took it!"

"I'm the sheriff of Ash Fork and this man is my deputy. Who took what from you?"

"Them fellas driving a small band of tall horses about two miles back. They got the drop on me and made me step away from the wagon while they took whatever they could carry on horseback."

"I'm sorry for your misfortune," Ruff said, reining in High Man. "They stole five of our best Thoroughbred mares from a barn down in Ash Fork. We're trying to catch up with them and get our mares back."

"They got them mares heavy with foal." The driver spat a stream of tobacco into the blowing wind. "Are there just the four of you on their trail?"

Sheriff Holt said, "That's right. How many horse thieves are we following?"

"Five," the driver said without hesitation. "All

of them well armed and mean looking. I was sure they was going to shoot me and steal this wagon. I thought I was a goner."

"How did the mares look?" Ruff asked. "Are they laboring?"

"I was thinking I might be killed so I didn't rightly notice. I can tell you the horses all looked played out. Heads down in the wind, tails whipped up between their back legs and ice on their coats. But like I said, I was just worried I was gonna be shot and my wagon took by 'em. I was hopin' to be let go so I could drive on to Prescott same as I do every month."

"Did they say anything about where they were headed?" the deputy asked.

The driver managed a humorless chuckle. "Hell no! What kind of dumb thieves tell you where they are goin'?"

"Can you tell us anything that might help us when we catch up with them?" Houston shouted, his words snatched away by the gusting wind. "Anything at all."

"Just that they were a mean looking bunch and I had the feeling they were thinking about ventilating my carcass for the hell of it. One of them argued to leave me dead and turn my wagon around and head west." The freighter took a deep breath then added, "But another one said that if they took my wagon and mules then they were sure to be overtaken, caught and hanged. I was by-gawd quick to agree!"

"How far is the next town?" Houston asked.

The sheriff answered before the freighter could. "I rode through it a couple of years ago. It's about five miles. It's called Rocky Gorge and it's just a couple of saloons, a flea infested hotel and two cafes. That's probably where the men we're chasing figure to hole up for tonight."

"Mister," Ruff asked, "does Rocky Gorge have a livery with a barn?"

"Yep," the freighter said, "it's owned by a blacksmith who does damn fine work and has helped me out a time or two. You'll be there before dark, and I'd guess that there's a good chance that's where your horses and the thieves will be found. Now, if you've no more questions I'd sure like to get on down to deliver what I have left to Fort Whipple. I'm a couple hours behind schedule and I won't get there before sundown."

"Thanks for your help," Sheriff Holt told the driver who cracked his whip and set his mules back into motion.

The sheriff touched spurs to the flank of his horse. "We'll ride into Rocky Gorge and head for that livery barn. The men we're chasin' will most likely be in the saloon and we can figure out a plan before we brace them."

"I already have a simple but effective plan." Houston laid his gloved hand on the butt of his gun.

The sheriff said something, but his words were snatched away in the wind and Ruff figured they weren't worth hearing anyways.

Back in the hotel, Darby Buckingham finished his medium rare steak along with a second glass of French wine. He smacked his lips with satisfaction and lit a Cuban cigar then leaned back at his table and surveyed the dining room that was half-filled with collection of people he would never know or have much interest in meeting. They were a mix of what he supposed were primarily merchants and businessmen. Several were already drunk and loud, their laughter sounding like the braying of a donkeys while others were huddled together at small tables, speaking in whispers as if they were settling the world's most important matters.

Just a few tables away, a pair of men had gotten into a heated argument and were cussing each other out at the tops of their voices. Darby wished they'd go outside to settle their differences. Suddenly, the much larger of the pair, a heavy-set and ugly man wearing a silk shirt and frock coat, threw a punch that knocked his smaller opponent completely out of his chair. The big man then jumped on the downed man's chest and everyone in the room heard the sound of the smaller man's expelled breath and saw his face turn ghost white. Darby, having been a champion bare-knuckles fighter, knew the man on the floor was immediately defenseless and in bad shape.

"You cheatin' bastard, you seduced my wife with lies and promises when I was out of town! You can have the cheatin' bitch and good riddance! She's yours!"

The smaller man on the bottom, quite dapper and handsome and with the look of a professional gambler, was nearly unconscious, but that didn't stop the big man from pounding his victim's face twice with heavy blows. To Darby's experienced eye, it seemed likely that the one who had been wronged might kill the helpless Lothario.

"Enough!" Darby bellowed, placing his cigar down on a platter and then going over to stop the brutal beating. "He's finished!"

"Stay out of this because I'm going to beat him to death!"

Darby reached down and locked his right arm around the big man's bull neck and yanked him to his feet. He shoved the man away and raised his fists. "You've exacted more than enough revenge."

"I'll decide when I'm finished!"

"No," Darby said quietly, "I'll decide, and I say this is finished."

The big man lunged at Darby throwing a roundhouse right. It was a terrible idea. Darby blocked the wild punch with his left forearm and drove an uppercut into the man's protruding belly so hard that everyone in the room heard the explosive whoosh of suddenly expelled breath. The big man dropped to his knees, then grabbed the edge of a table and slowly hauled himself erect. He stared at Darby for a moment, then snatched a wicked looking steak knife off the table. "I'm gonna gut you!" he croaked.

"Drop the knife and crawl out of here," Darby ordered, "before you eat your teeth."

The man staggered forward swinging the knife. Darby easily sidestepped his attacker and clubbed him alongside the jaw, the blow sounded like a heavy limb breaking as he knocked the man out cold.

One of the other diners came over and said, "You

might have broke Mr. Patterson's jaw."

"He's lucky I didn't break his neck. Now he'll have to speak through clenched teeth and not many will be able to understand his words."

"Mr. Patterson has a lot of friends in this town, mister. They'll be coming at you soon enough."

"Who's the one he almost killed?" Darby asked, looking over at the poor fellow who was spitting blood and trying to stand.

"He's a gambler named Charley Johnson who is just passing through for a few days. He has a way with women and ... well, this time he chose the wrong one to fool around with."

The Derby Man went over and lifted him up and sat him in a chair. He doused a napkin with water from his drinking glass and wiped the blood from the man's once handsome face.

The gambler's eyes were nearly swollen shut and filled with pain.

"Mr. Johnson, if I were you, I'd find Mrs. Patterson and get out of town with her fast," Darby suggested. "I won't be here tomorrow and there wasn't anyone else making a move to save you."

Johnson could barely manage to whisper. "I love sweet Peaches but she don't love me. She's just desperate to escape her husband and who could blame her? Now she's the one that needs protecting."

"Well," Darby said, "you're certainly not up to that."

"I have to be," Charlie Johnson managed to say. "Patterson is likely to beat poor Peaches to death sooner or later!"

There is sure a lot of sadness and trouble here in

Ash Fork, Darby thought with a shake of his head, *probably because of bad times and bad weather. Be good to get to Prescott and to see Dolly Beavers again.*

Darby retrieved his Cuban cigar and headed upstairs to his room turning his worried mind back on Dolly Beavers. The general tenor of the letter had been especially troubling because Dolly was, by her nature, a very happy person with an adventurous and fun-loving spirit. Dolly wasn't particularly bright, and she certainly wasn't well educated, but then she never pretended to be anything other than always being fun, good and honest. Furthermore, she was devoted to him and he had very much missed her on this latest trip to find and research a new story. Dolly had fine penmanship and copied every word of his manuscripts so that he had his own original manuscript to keep safe while he sent Dolly's reproduction off to his New York City publisher.

Up in his room Darby poured a shot of cognac and once more pondered what might have been troubling Dolly when she wrote her letter only a couple of weeks before. His dark thoughts were interrupted by a knock on his door. Thinking it might be some of Patterson's friends out to get revenge, Darby reached for his derringer and made sure it was ready to fire.

"Who is it!" he asked loudly.

"Sir! May I have a word with you?" came the reply. "My name is Homer Gentry and I'm this town's mayor as well as the editor of the weekly *Ash Fork Sentinel.* I met with your friend, Miss Ballou, and helped her out in exchange for what I hope will be an interview. If it's too late in the evening, I'll be happy to come calling tomorrow morning. I'll buy you breakfast in exchange for an interview if you would be so kind."

Darby Buckingham was not at all above enjoying a little flattery and he was still fully dressed and wide awake. After a fight, it had always been difficult to go right to sleep, so he opened his door.

"Come in. Would you like a glass of cognac?" he offered. "It's not the best, but it's passable."

"How very kind of you, Mr. Buckingham."

Darby judged the Ash Fork editor to be a man in his early sixties and from the frayed and well-worn condition of Gentry's suit, Darby figured the man was not at all prosperous. Small wonder because from what he'd seen of the town's populous, he doubted even half the citizens of Ash Fork could read or write.

"Mr. Buckingham, I understand you were involved in a scuffle downstairs only a short while ago."

"I was." A pause. "I really had no choice. Mr. Patterson was beating a smaller man half to death."

"Was it over Patterson's wife, Peaches?" the Gentry asked.

"Yes," Darby replied. "Apparently he had been cuckolded by the loser of the fight, a handsome gambler named Charley Johnson."

The editor nodded with understanding. "Mr. Patterson is insanely jealous. He owns the mercantile and is prosperous, but he is much disliked and never waits on customers. His wife, Peaches, is extremely popular. She's young enough to be her husband's daughter. I'm afraid his jealous rage has happened before. I warned Peaches not to marry him, but she was having a hard time and knew Patterson would never let her end up in a saloon or whorehouse."

"I see."

"And what you did to him in the dining room downstairs will be talked about in Ash Fork for years. In fact, it will make you a legend. I can't tell you how delighted people around here will be about Patterson finally getting knocked out cold by one tremendous punch."

"The foul bully swore he's done with his young, beautiful wife."

The editor waved a hand dismissively. "He'll always take her back. She's his obsession and someday he'll get himself killed in a jealous rage."

"I've seen that happen before."

"But enough of our town troubles," the mayor and editor said, pulling out a well-used notebook. "Please tell me all about yourself, Mr. Buckingham. I've read a number of your dime novels and ..."

"Which one is your favorite?" Darby asked, setting a trap in case this man was flattering him with a lie.

"I loved *Silver Shot,* but my favorite is probably *The Comstock Camels.* Did you really win a camel in Virginia City and then enter it in a race down to Goldfield?"

"I did, and that was a fiasco! One of the worst experiences of my life," Darby said with a rueful chuckle. "I should have just sold or even given the beast away and cut my losses, but it made for a great novel ... at my own considerable expense and humiliation."

Gentry laughed. "So I gathered! You have had some remarkable adventures since coming to the West. I take it that your faithful and constant companion, Miss Dolly Beavers, is not with you?"

"She is waiting for me in Prescott," Darby said, leaving it at that.

"I would have loved to have met her. My wife Irma has a heart of pure gold. We have three children ... but we sent them to Prescott to school. This town is no place to raise children, but Irma misses them very much and so do I. If my newspaper goes broke ... and it very well might before spring, we'll move to Prescott. You know, there are a few fine people in Ash Fork, but most here are ruthless and thieves, beginning with the man you knocked out cold downstairs. And everyone is trying to cash in on the coming railroad."

"If Patterson has money and owns a thriving mercantile, why would he resort to thievery?"

The editor sampled his cognac. "It has been my experience in life that the more money a man has, the more he wants. And Mr. Patterson has a lot of money. He makes more by hiring a gang of thieves both here and even in Old Mexico. They steal and deliver to his big mercantile where he re-sells the goods at unbeatable prices and still makes a considerable profit."

"What does Sheriff Holt and his deputy do about this ongoing injustice?"

"Just between us, they do nothing because they are being bribed."

"That's outrageous!"

"Yes," Gentry sadly agreed. "And as for the stolen goods, think about it. Mr. Patterson's customers buy stolen goods at a discount, so why would they complain?"

"Exactly what kind of stolen goods does he deal in?" Darby asked, not really very curious because he was hoping to put Ash Fork quickly behind him.

"Guns, ammunition, expensive items like good saddles, horses and ..."

"Wait," Darby interrupted. "Did you say horses?"

"Yes. He might, for instance, have good horses stolen in Mexico and brought up here for resale at a fine profit. Same with other things ... whatever he can make a tidy profit at, with Sheriff Holt and his corrupt deputy taking a small cut of the profits."

"Now that *is* interesting," Darby mused. "You know that the Ballou people had five of their Thoroughbreds stolen last night?"

"So I heard," Gentry said, "but there is no proof that Sheriff Holt or his deputy had anything to do with that."

"But they *might* have," Darby pressed. "And if they did, the two Ballou brothers who left with them this morning could be riding into a death trap."

Homer Gentry's expression suddenly darkened with worry. "I hadn't thought of that, but you're right and with the weather being what is there isn't a thing we can do to warn them."

Darby's drummed his fingers on the arms of his chair with impatience. "If the sheriff and his deputy do turn against Ruff and Houston, they will either be shot dead by the brothers or I will bring them to justice, one way or another."

For a few moments, the two sat brooding and then Gentry said, "Mr. Buckingham, please tell me what kind of a punch you delivered to do so much damage to a man the size of Mr. Patterson."

"I blocked his looping overhand right, ducked my shoulder and put all my power into a right uppercut," Darby explained. "The man he has no real skills as a pugilist."

"But you do."

"I was a well-known heavyweight champion when I lived back in New York," Darby said modestly. He frowned, turning his mind to Ruff and Houston who were in pursuit of horse thieves and he couldn't help and deeply concerned that the Tennessee horsemen were in grave danger.

"Mr. Buckingham, since there is nothing we can do but hope for the best, would you tell me just a little more about the years of your bare-knuckles fighting. And before that during your time as a circus strongman?"

"That was quite a few years ago," Darby admitted. "But I still do lifting to keep up my strength."

Dixie knocked on the door and then entered. "I don't want to interrupt this interview," she said, turning to leave.

"Don't give it a thought," Gentry said quickly. "I can continue tomorrow morning when we have breakfast."

The mayor and editor tossed down his cognac. "Mr. Buckingham, thank you for the drink and the start of a good story."

"We can continue our talk over breakfast," Darby promised, distracted by his worry over Dixie's beloved brothers. But since there was nothing that could be done to warn them of the sheriff and his deputy's possible duplicity, there was no use in telling Dixie what he'd just learned from Homer Gentry.

Dixie had enough to worry about already… *hell,* Darby thought, *we all do.*

CHAPTER 9

"There it is," Sheriff Holt said in the fading light, as warm vapor clouds floated out of his mouth. "Rocky Gorge."

"It ain't much," Cletus said contemptuously while slapping his gloved hands together. "Sheriff, how do you want this handled?"

"We'll circle around and ride the back alley through town and come up to that big barn on the north end. That's has to be where we'll find your mares."

"They might have a guard or two in the barn," Houston said. "I would if I stole 'em."

"Possible, but unlikely," Sheriff Holt responded. "It'll be like a freezer box in that barn and I don't expect anyone would want to stay there through a night this cold."

"I guess we just ride up and find out," Ruff said tightly. "I'm ready to put an end to this manhunt."

"Me too," Houston agreed.

"All right," the sheriff finally agreed, "just

remember that I'm the one who is running this show, and no one shoots until I shoot."

Ruff and Houston both had other ideas, but it was so cold and windy that they didn't seem worth debating at the moment.

"Cletus," Holt said, "you and me are going in first."

"The hell with that!" Houston challenged. "Those are Ballou mares."

The sheriff started to say something, but Cletus spoke first. "Sheriff, these rebel boys got a point. I figure they surely do deserve to go in first."

Both Ruff and Houston were surprised to hear the deputy stand up for them and even more surprised when the sheriff drew his six-gun. "Okay, fine, but remember, if there is anyone inside you don't just gun them down, but instead order 'em to surrender."

"We sure as hell will and I'm glad you are finally seeing things the right way," Houston growled as he dismounted and also drew his gun.

Ruff led the two Thoroughbred stallions over to a fence and tied them up. If shooting started, he wanted High Man and High Fire to be well out of the way of gunfire.

"I'm ready if you are, Brother."

They moved carefully through the snow and up to the big barn door then eased it open. Inside, with the aid of flickering lamp light, they saw two men wrapped in blankets drinking from a bottle.

"Freeze!" Houston shouted, taking aim.

Both horse thieves dropped their blankets, but not their precious bottle of whiskey.

Sheriff Holt and his deputy were now inside with

their guns trained on the horse thieves. "Where are your friends?" Holt demanded, looking around in case any of them were in the hay sleeping or hiding.

The shorter man said, "Most likely they're holed up nice and warm with saloon women."

"You're under arrest for stealing those mares," Holt said. "Stand up then turn around slow and easy and put your hands behind your backs."

Ruff watched as Cletus tied their wrists up with rope.

"Lash 'em to that post," Holt ordered. "And then let's find get the rest of 'em."

"Shouldn't be too hard," the deputy answered.

Minutes later, Sheriff Holt marched up the street with his gun in his fist while Ruff and Houston followed close behind with Cletus plodding along in the rear.

As they neared the saloon, Houston leaned in close to his brother. "There are only three left to face. Better odds than I'd dare hope for."

"We'll just see how this plays out," Ruff said in a low voice.

Even over the wind, Ruff could hear piano music and the sound of loud and boisterous laughter. He stayed just behind the sheriff as the lawman stepped quickly through the doorway.

It was dim inside, but there was just enough light to see the silhouettes of men strung along the bar and some others sitting hunched over card tables.

"Everyone, freeze!" Sheriff Holt shouted.

The piano music stopped and so did the laughter and loud talk.

"I'm the sheriff of Ash Fork. Me and my deputy have two horse thieves tied up in the barn and I'm lookin' for three more! I'm gonna find out who you are so you might as well come forward."

Nobody moved, not even the bartender with a raised bottle in his fist.

Ruff stepped up beside the sheriff. "It's our mares that were stole in Ash Fork and by damned, I'm going to make sure whichever of you took them faces justice!"

For a moment, there was just a stillness and then a man at the bar went for his gun. Ruff and Sheriff Holt both shot him at the same moment and his body slammed into the bar before crashing to the floor.

An instant later a man who had been playing poker at one of the back tables jumped up from his chair and fired, his bullet striking the sheriff in the chest and knocking him down. Houston's gun boomed and his bullet tore through the poker player's forehead.

A split-second later, a third man wearing only dirty underwear burst out of a back room using a chubby and very naked prostitute as a shield. He had his arm around her neck in a chokehold and a gun in his free hand. He pressed the Colt to the side of the woman's head and yelled, "If you try to shoot me, I'll blow her brains out!"

The prostitute wailed and struggled but she was held tight and was trembling violently in fear.

"Jude," the bartender shouted at the almost naked man, "let Olive go!"

But Jude shook his head. "She's the only chance I

have now and I ain't nearly dumb enough to let her loose so I can hang!"

Ruff glanced down at Sheriff Holt as the badly wounded lawman battled for his life.

Houston dropped on one knee beside the sheriff then pressed his palm hard down on the wound while trying to keep his revolver up and ready to fire. "He's goin' fast, Ruff. I don't think I can save him."

"Mister," Ruff shouted, "let the woman go and we'll take you back to stand trial. Do it right goddamn now!"

Jude choked Olive's neck even tighter and her face was turning blue while her struggles were becoming feeble.

Houston glanced up at Ruff who took a deep breath and then he saw Cletus pushing between them.

"Deputy, your sheriff is dying!"

In reply, Burr coolly glanced down and shot Sheriff Holt in the head then he turned his gun on Ruff. He fired and a bullet creased Ruff's skull and caused him to lose his balance.

Houston spun around on his knee and threw himself at Ruff, knocking him sideways and causing the deputy's next bullet to fly wide of its target. Ruff's head bounced off a table and he momentarily lost consciousness. At the same time, Houston managed to empty his gun. His first bullet entered the Ash Fork deputy's skull just under the man's jaw and blew off the back of his ugly head.

Lying on the floor, Ruff shook his head desperately trying to clear his vision.

At just that moment, when everyone in the saloon

was starting at Ruff and his brother, Judd hurled Olive aside. In three quick steps he was halfway across the saloon with his gun pointed at Ruff when the bartender's double-barreled shotgun blew Judd nearly in half.

Ruff didn't clearly remember what happened next because he lost consciousness again. Sometime later he heard loud shouts and then boots pounding on the floor and Houston's distant voice telling him not to try and get up yet.

"Are you alright, Brother?"

"I reckon I've felt better."

"I told the men in here I'd buy drinks on the house if they hanged that pair in the barn. Bartender thought that was a damned good idea. So they left to get it done."

"How long have I been out cold?"

"About an hour. I bandaged that head and I can tell you that Dixie won't be impressed."

"And Sheriff Holt?"

"He's dead along with Cletus."

"I can't understand why he'd shoot his own cousin."

"Cletus was probably was in on the stealing of our horses and hadn't bothered to tell Holt about it. My guess is that he was also tired of playing second fiddle to the sheriff and wanted a bigger share of the money from the sale of our mares."

"What a mess!" Ruff said, allowing his brother to help him to his feet.

"You got a nasty crease across the side of your skull."

"It'll heal and the bleeding will stop soon enough in this freezing weather."

"I expect that's true."

Just then a half dozen of the saloon's customers hurried inside and told everyone that they'd earned free drinks. The bartender let out a sigh. "What about the dead sheriff, his deputy and the five horse thieves we just laid out on the boardwalk?"

"We'll take Sheriff Holt's body back to Ash Fork and he'll get a proper burial," Houston said loudly as he extracted a thin roll of money for the drinks he'd promised. "For all I care you can drag the rest of their bodies into the mountain and let them feed the bears and wolves."

"Might do that. Ground is too hard frozen to dig graves for the likes of that bunch. I got some hot chili and beef on the fire and I'll find you men beds upstairs for the night."

"Appreciate that," Ruff told the man. "And we'll take a sample of that whiskey we're paying for tonight."

The bartender nodded. "We'll be talking about what happened here clear into next summer, I reckon. Sure glad that Olive didn't get her brains blown out ... she's one of our favorite girls. And that was one hell of a gunfight."

Late the next afternoon in Ash Fork, Darby Buckingham, Dixie and Mrs. Peaches Patterson stood outside and watched the buckboard led by Houston and driven by Ruff as it came rolling slowly up the muddy, half-frozen street. Lying inside the buckboard for anyone to see was Sheriff Holt's stiff body and tied to the back of the buckboard were their string of very weary Thoroughbred mares.

"We got it done," Houston said, dismounting and taking a deep breath. "Ruff about got himself killed and the deputy shot the sheriff dead. Lot of blood and some got hanged. But it's all over now."

Peaches Patterson swallowed hard. She ignored her husband's garbled command to come back into their general store and watch over the counter and the money. With Patterson's jaw broken, his words were slurred, but still understandable.

"Gawdamn you, get in here right now or I'll knock the hell outa you!" Patterson stormed, bursting outside, then hauling up short as he saw what was causing all the commotion out in the street.

"What happened out there?" he asked, lowering his voice.

Darby Buckingham heard the question and looked over at the big man he'd knocked out only a couple of days earlier. Like Patterson and everyone else in Ash Fork, he desperately wanted to know what had happened on the hunt for the horse thieves and what had gone so tragically wrong.

Darby lit a cigar and headed for the buckboard.

Peaches rushed after him before her husband could grab her.

"Get back in here, girl, or I'll blister your hide!"

Peaches slipped her arm through Darby Buckingham's and whispered, "I'm really gonna get whipped now."

"What happened to Charley the gambler?" Darby

asked. "Why didn't you run off with him?"

"He didn't amount to anything much," Peaches hissed, "no sense makin' one mistake right on top of another mistake, is there?"

"I guess not," Darby said as his attention turned back to Dixie and Ruff. "This just turned into one hell of a sad mess."

Peaches had auburn colored hair, a slight dimple in her cheeks and a face that would catch the eye of any man. She pursed her lips, glanced back over her shoulder and whispered, "Mr. Buckingham, I know this is a terrible, terrible time to ask, but when are you leaving for Prescott?"

"Tomorrow morning."

"If I ain't beat to death by my husband before then, could I please go with you?"

The earnestness of her words turned the Derby Man full around in the mud and he stared at the beautiful, but obviously desperate young woman. Their eyes locked for just a moment and then Darby heard himself say, "Yes you can, Miss Patterson. And I won't let your husband do you harm or stop you. Go up and sleep tonight in Dixie's room. I'll make sure she understands why."

"Thank you! No more calling me Mrs. Patterson, from now on please just call me plain old Peaches."

"Miss Peaches, there is nothing old or plain about you."

"How sweet of you to say that! Just one more thing," Peaches quickly added as she twisted around and stuck her tongue out at her enraged husband. "Is either of those two tall Ballou brothers married yet?"

"No," Darby said, suppressing a grin.

"I sure am glad to hear that!" Peaches squealed before heading back inside the hotel. Over at his general store, her wealthy but miserable husband stomped and hollered but no one in Ash Fork bothered to listen.

CHAPTER 10

"The buggy is hitched up and ready to roll," Houston said early the next morning. "It's a nice rig but we'll have to move smartly in order to reach Prescott before dark."

"That's music to my ears," Darby replied. "It seems like a year since I left New Mexico."

"It has been eventful," Houston agreed. "Say, I understand that Miss Peaches Patterson is leaving with us bound for Prescott."

"That's right. I think she's making a good decision. That brutish husband of hers is really dangerous."

"You'd think that after you broke his jaw, he'd have learned some humility, but I guess not."

"Some men never learn anything. Let's get out of here."

"Oh, Mr. Buckingham! May I speak with you for just a moment?"

Darby turned to see Homer Gentry, the town's editor and mayor who was hurrying toward him.

"I just wanted to say goodbye and wish you all the

best," the slightly out of breath editor said. "And to thank you for giving that wonderful interview. I'm going to sell a lot of newspapers and create plenty of new readers for your novels."

"In that case we both win. Good luck, Mr. Gentry. It has been a pleasure talking to you and I hope you figure out a way to leave Ash Fork ... only because I think you could do far better elsewhere."

"Funny you should say that," the mayor and newspaper man said with a smile. "My missus and I were talking last night, and we agreed to relocate as soon as my term of office is over in Ash Fork next month. I have a friend in Prescott who owns the *Arizona Miner* and he's asked me several times in the past if I would consider buying into the newspaper and becoming his partner. I've decided to accept, and if you wouldn't mind, please stop by and tell him I'll be there in about four weeks."

"I'll be happy to do that," Darby said. "Why the sudden change of mind?"

"Well," Gentry said, "as you may or may not know, Prescott was our first territorial capital for ten years, but lost that title to Tucson."

"I think I might have heard something about that."

"Prescott won it back and now the capital is built in the town plaza and the town is growing fast. Mining isn't the only major employer anymore, but it is still significant. Government, livestock and timber have become very important to Prescott so, unlike Ash Fork, its economy is quite robust and diversified."

"I see. But what about all that opportunity coming

Ash Fork's way with the railroad's plans?"

"That may not happen for a few more years. My friend's Prescott newspaper has outgrown its office. I'll bring my printing press down to the capital and we'll find a bigger office right downtown, probably on Gurley or Granite Street."

Homer Gentry stood a little taller. "I'm in my mid-sixties now and having a partner and more opportunity will be very important to me at the tail end of my long career."

"That's wonderful news, Mr. Gentry."

"Homer." The newspaper man stuck out his hand. "Thank you and I look forward to seeing you in Prescott very soon ... and getting a new interview for the *Arizona Miner?*"

"Of course!" He was about to say more but, suddenly, his words were cut off by a shrill cry. "Mr. Buckingham, help me!"

Darby turned to see Peaches rush out of the hotel. She looked gorgeous but also scared out of her wits and an instant later he saw the reason for the young woman's fear. Her husband had a gun in his big fist and he was coming after his young wife with murder in his eye.

"Oh my," the editor said, "this is not looking good for anyone!"

"Homer, get off the street," Darby ordered as Peaches raced to the Derby Man and flung her arms around his waist crying, "Help me!"

"Let go of me so I can move," Darby said quietly. "And slide in behind me. I make a wide shield."

Peaches released her hold on him, and Darby

reached inside his coat pocket for his derringer. It was, of course, no match for the revolver in Patterson's fist but it was all he had, and he meant to make a stand.

"Patterson, hold up!" Darby shouted, raising the palm of his left hand outward. "If you kill either of us you will hang!"

"I'm going to kill you and then I'm going to kill that cheatin' bitch behind you!"

Darby waited just as long as possible. He had two shots and neither one would be accurate beyond twenty feet. Patterson knew that was his big advantage and so at twenty or thirty feet away he stopped, planted his feet, took aim and fired at the exact same moment Darby opened fire.

The volley was loud and deadly. Darby swore he felt a bullet's breeze pass his cheek. Peaches screamed. Dixie, who had just emerged from the hotel with her bag, dropped it, drew her six-gun and fired in one smooth motion. Her shot had only traveled about fifty feet, but it was perfect and blew a hole through Patterson's chest piercing both lungs.

The big man fell and coughed blood into the mud.

For a long moment, there was a hushed silence.

"Oh my god!" Peaches gasped, her expression changing from terror to joy. "He's finally dead! I'm now a . . . a *rich* widow!"

Darby shoved his derringer back into his coat pocket and took a deep breath before asking, "Do you still want to leave Ash Fork with us?"

It only took Peaches a moment to decide. "I certainly was looking forward to getting to know those Ballou brothers much, much better. But now, since I'm the only heir to all of my late husband's holdings ... well, sir, don't you agree that it would be very, very foolish of me to just ... just walk away from all of my late husband's property and money?"

Darby couldn't believe what he was hearing, but he supposed it really did make sense from the young woman's point of view.

"Peaches, at the very least you should stay and run the business," he told her. "You can always sell out later."

"I think that is exactly what I should do," Peaches told Darby as she reached up on her toes and kissed his cheek. "That's for your bravery. I shall never forget it."

Darby looked toward the hotel and studied Dixie. Her face was a little pale, but her hand was steady as she holstered her revolver. "What about Dixie? I'm not sure which of us killed your husband ... maybe both. But if she hadn't ..."

"Oh, I *will* thank her too!" Peaches exclaimed. "And I'll even let her have anything she wants from my store."

"Fitting," Darby said. "Very fitting."

Darby left Peaches and went to stand over Patterson's body a moment before continuing on to Dixie. He touched the young horsewoman's arm and asked, "Are you alright?"

Dixie raised her chin. "Yes ... yes I am. It's just that I never killed a human before."

"He was a very violent and dangerous man," Darby reminded the girl from Tennessee.

Dixie was silent for a few moments, then blurted, "Darby, do you reckon it my shot or yours that killed him?"

"Both," Darby said without hesitation. "I fired twice, but only hit him once in the belly. He was already as good as dead when your bullet pierced his lungs and possibly even his heart. In short, you just put him out of a lot of misery, but the fool was already dying."

Darby didn't know if that was exactly true, but he felt it might make Dixie feel a little better, so that's why he explained it that way.

"Anyway, Peaches has decided to remain here in Ash Fork and she wants to reward your bravery just now by offering you the chance to have anything you want from *her* store."

"I could *never* take blood money."

"I killed him; you just put him out of his misery."

Dixie expelled a deep breath. "Did she really mean I could have anything in that mercantile?"

"Yes, and you deserve it, Dixie. I am not unaware that you not only helped to save her life, but my own as well so we are really both in your debt."

"When you put it that way, I think I will take up her offer. I've been inside that big mercantile and there are many wonderful things I'd love to own."

"Such as?"

"A new and limited-edition Winchester rifle," Dixie said without hesitation.

"Then you deserve and shall have it." Darby motioned for Peaches to join them. "Miss Ballou wants the limited-edition Winchester rifle."

Peaches didn't hesitate for even an instant. "Good, and I'll even throw in a box of ammunition!"

"Deal," Dixie said, finally managing a smile.

A few minutes later, Ruff and Houston arrived and took in the situation at a glance. People were coming out to stand around Patterson's body and Darby did not see a single tear shed.

"Nice shooting, dude!"

Darby turned to Houston. "If you'll look closely, there are two bullet holes in the man. Only one is mine."

"And the other?"

"Your sister," Darby said quietly. "Don't tell her this, but I think her shot hit Patterson first. I just got him on the way down."

The brothers nodded, faces grim. Ruff asked, "And this doesn't change anything?"

"Peaches isn't coming with us now. She just inherited the mercantile and I suspect some other valuable properties and a lot of cash."

"Damn," Houston muttered. "I'm glad she's free now, but I was sure looking forward to getting to know her better."

"Well," Darby said, "into every life a little rain must fall."

"Amen to that," Ruff agreed, heading for the mercantile.

Houston frowned. "I was just getting my mind set on … well, how I'd have time in Prescott to get to know Peaches a whole lot better."

"I'm sure there will be plenty of other lovely young women in Prescott," Darby assured Houston. "And since it is only a long day's ride away, you can pay Peaches frequent romantic visits."

"Well," Houston said, a slow grin creeping across his handsome face, "that really is a fine way to look at the new situation!"

Funny, the Derby Man thought, as he reached for a notebook and pencil, *how unpredictable things sometimes turn out to be. Wonderful material for a new novel mainly set right here in Ash Fork.*

CHAPTER 11

The territorial capital of Arizona was well situated in a huge valley surrounded on three sides by snow-dusted mountains that fed into Granite Creek. There were pine forests on Granite and Spruce Mountains and the elevation was at a year-round and weather-pleasant 5,300 feet. As Darby and the Ballou family came down the valley from Ash Fork, they passed Fort Whipple, a military post located just north of the town on Granite Creek. They saw a herd of cavalry horses grazing on rich grass and there was a breeze, so that United States flag was snapping sharply on a westerly wind.

The air was crisp and clear at this higher altitude and they could see the mountains dotted with cabins and small mines. As they got closer to Prescott itself, they saw that the main structures of the territorial capital were the imposing governor's mansion, the capitol building and the Montezuma Hotel. There were dozens of homesteads with dry fields of corn and hay and cattle by the hundreds foraging for winter feed.

"I like the looks of it," Dixie said to Darby. "Good feed and water and flat ground for pastures and a racetrack. Enough timber within easy reach off the mountains to build both fences and structures, plus the air is clear and pine-scented."

Darby nodded in agreement. He had not spoken much since leaving Ash Fork because his mind was now locked on what might be amiss in Dolly Beaver's life. He would soon find out, because although there were several thousand people here, it wouldn't be hard to find a woman like Dolly. Anyone who saw her did not soon forget her.

"You're worried about your lady friend, aren't you?" Dixie said, glancing at the Derby Man and noting his grim expression.

"I am. You know, uncertainty is often more troubling to the mind than the reality. We always tend to fix upon the worst possible outcome."

"I know. I do that too."

On the southeast corner of Goodwin and Montezuma streets they found the big Plaza Stables and Shoeing Shop with a large, well-kept barn for their Thoroughbreds. The owner wasn't on the property but a quiet young man of about sixteen who was feeding horses and looked to be part Indian told them about a couple of nearby hotels.

"Do you or someone stay with the horses all night so that no one can steal them?" Ruff asked.

"My name is Mando Parker and I stay here all the time. I'll watch over your fine horses, so no worries."

To show that he was serious about his promise,

Mando stepped over to a stall and emerged with a double-barreled shotgun. "I hit what I aim at," he said in a serious tone of voice.

Darby had to smile because he could have said exactly the same. "Where can I buy a shotgun like that, Mando?"

"The Bashford Mercantile on Gurley Street carries them."

"Thanks, and the best hotel?"

Mando shrugged. "Take your pick, sir. There is the Montezuma Hotel on Montezuma Street, the Sherman House close by and the Hassayampa Hotel on Gurley Street. They are good places. Too expensive for me, but not for you, I think."

"Thank you."

Less than fifteen minutes later, they were standing in the lobby of the Montezuma Hotel and Darby asked the desk clerk if he knew a Miss Dolly Beavers.

"Sure I do! She's not one to let her presence go unnoticed, that's for certain."

"Is she staying here?"

"She did when she first arrived but then she bought a nice little house just a few blocks off the plaza."

"Is she ... all right?"

The man blinked, then chose his words carefully. "If you mean health-wise, she's fine. She walks around the plaza a couple of times every morning with that half-breed girl she's protecting."

It was Darby's turn to be surprised and he blurted, "Could you kindly direct me to her residence?"

"Sure, go up to Union Street and turn right. Her house stands out like a sore thumb. She had it painted ... *pink."*

"Pink?" Darby asked, hoping he'd heard incorrectly.

"Yep. And I can tell you that a lot of her neighbors are upset. To satisfy them she had the trim painted blue, but the place still looks like a high-toned brothel, if you ask me."

"Well, she does love colors," Darby sheepishly admitted.

"Oh, yeah, and she loves roses. She's got some beauties, and she and that pretty half-breed girl are always out in the garden tending to them and the other flowers. People didn't like the color she had painted on her cottage, but Miss Beavers is so friendly and ... well, easy on the eyes ... that no one could stay mad at her except the ones that are out to get Mando and his sister, Reba."

Darby Buckingham's smile melted. "I met Mando at the livery. He seems like a good lad."

"He works hard, keeps to himself and doesn't say much to anyone. But ... well, it's a long and not very pleasant story, and I'm sure it would be better if Miss Beavers explained it herself."

"I'll go to see her at once."

"What about a room?"

"I've just decided that I'll probably be staying elsewhere."

"With Miss Beavers?"

Darby said nothing.

The hotel clerk was in his thirties, well dressed and professional but his curiosity overrode his judgement and he blurted, "Sir, are you her husband ... or maybe a brother?"

"I'm a dear *friend,"* Darby replied, not wishing to say more for the tongue-wagging people who loved to gossip.

A few minutes later with manuscript pouch and bags in hand, Darby Buckingham marched up Union Street and there it was ... a cute pink cottage with red, and yellow roses blooming in wild profusion. The place had a freshly painted purple picket fence and Darby studied it for several minutes, thinking it certainly was an eye-catching house, although it appeared that a few of the front windows were broken out and boarded up.

Odd about those windows, Darby thought. *Very troubling, actually.*

He was about to open the gate when Dolly appeared with a nice-looking, part Indian girl. He remembered that she was Mando's sister and the resemblance was plain for anyone to see. The girl had long black hair, shiny as a raven's wing and tied back with a colorful bow. She was only a little over five feet tall and her complexion was the color of soft buckskin. She had a nice laugh, too, as something funny passed between her and Dolly. It was instantly clear that there was nothing physically wrong with Dolly, she was as perky and pretty as ever.

"Hello, my dear!" Darby called.

Dolly had been holding a pair of pruning shears but suddenly she let out a squeal, tossed the shears up into the air and charged forward to throw her arms around the Derby Man.

"Oh, sweet Dumpling Darby! I thought you might never get here! It has taken you *so long!*"

"It's been a challenging journey," he admitted. "A lot of close calls and that sort of thing ... and although I'm a little worse for wear, I made it."

He leaned back and studied Dolly closely. He had not seen her in nearly six months, and she hadn't changed one bit except that she now had heightened color to her cheeks, probably from being out in the sun gardening. She was wearing a pretty bonnet and a plain dress that fit too tight. Dolly had always been a little top heavy, but he liked that, and she had a lovely face with large blue eyes and waterfalls of curly blonde hair. As he gazed into those blue eyes, he thought of all the times they had shared and how she had loved to be involved in researching his dime novels. Dolly Beavers had an adventuresome spirit and loved to travel.

He squeezed her tightly and planted a kiss on her full lips. She was not wearing her usual powerful perfume, but instead he detected the delicate scent of roses and it was pleasing and even sensuous.

"I'm so excited and I'll make you a wonderful dinner tonight with some of that whiskey that you love. I've been preparing for you, Honey Bunny!"

He cringed at the endearment but didn't have the heart to tell her that no man, much less a world champion fighter and former circus strong man, would care to be called Dumpling or Honey Bunny.

Dolly caressed his face lovingly and teased the curled tips of his thick black mustache. Finally, she removed his derby and ran her fingers lovingly though his hair.

"Ouch!"

Dolly recoiled with alarm and her expression turned to one of grave concern. "You have a wound on the back of your head, my big, beautiful panda bear!"

"It's healing," Darby sighed while patiently enduring the woman's sincere but utterly ridiculous endearments.

Dolly just loved to make up sweet names for him, but sometimes it really was too much. "I had a nasty accident. My stagecoach overturned on a steep, icy mountain road. The driver was killed but I was fortunate that some fine young horsemen from Tennessee happened to be coming along in a storm with ... oh, well, all that can be explained over dinner and drinks tonight."

"Of course," she said, raising her fingers to caress his scalp injury but Darby pulled back just in time saying, "Who is this lovely girl that I hear you have taken into your house?"

"This is Miss Reba Parker," Dolly said, beckoning the girl, who seemed quite shy, over to join them.

Reba was clearly of mixed blood and, like her brother Mando, rather handsome although too thin. She gave Darby a tenuous smile and a little curtsy and said, "I have heard much about you, Mr. Buckingham, Mister *Derby Man.*"

"All good, I hope," he said, pleased by the compliment.

"*Very* good. Miss Dolly, she loves you very much."

"As I love her. And I'm glad that she has had the pleasure of your company."

Reba's lips suddenly trembled and Darby was taken aback to see tears well up in her dark brown eyes.

"I'm sorry, did I say something wrong?"

"I bring Miss Dolly very much trouble," Reba confessed. "I should go live at the stable with Mando, but she will not let me go. She always worries about me."

Dolly said, "Like your journey from the New Mexico country, I'm sure that you would rather hear the story this evening after dinner, drinks and dessert."

"Dessert?" Darby asked, brightening. One of his main failings besides his expensive Cuban cigars and whiskey, was his sweet tooth.

"Yes, I will bake an apple pie this afternoon ... just the way you love them."

Darby almost had to struggle not to drool like a dim-witted fool. Dolly was a wonderful cook and when it came to baking cakes, pies and cookies, she played second fiddle to no woman.

"You look tired, my darling. Come sit on the porch and I'll bring us out cookies and lemonade."

"I wouldn't mind you spicing up the lemonade with some tequila or gin," he sighed, feeling an onrush of weariness from his long, difficult journey.

"Your wish is my command, Dumpling Cheeks."

Darby's eyes rolled but he managed to get up the stairs and plunk down in a comfortable rocking chair. There were some lovely cottonwood trees in front of Dolly's cottage and their leaves sparkled in the sun and danced on a soothing breeze. He saw neighbors peeking at him from behind windows and knew that his arrival would be a source of great interest and speculation.

Darby thought he might take a nap after the cookies and lemonade, and before he trudged on back to the Montezuma Hotel where Dixie, Ruff and Houston were rooming. He wanted to make sure that they knew where he was staying and were welcome to drop by soon and often.

Dolly loved company and he knew she would very much enjoy hearing about their exciting story of traveling all the way from Tennessee under the threat of a Confederate bounty. And although Dolly did not ride well, she looked marvelous in the saddle and loved horses. Darby was looking forward to escorting her over to the Plaza Stables and introducing her to the magnificent Ballou Thoroughbreds.

After dinner, Darby patted his stomach, lit a fresh Cuban and smiled with satisfaction. "Dolly, I haven't had that good a meal since last we were together. Now, would you like to go and sit out on the front porch and catch up on things? The weather is mild and ..."

"I don't think that would be a very good idea," Dolly said anxiously. "I try to stay indoors at night, and I keep my lights down low."

"Why don't you tell me what's going on here in Prescott. I already suspect it has something to do with you taking Reba into your home."

"It does," Dolly admitted. "And it is a rather long and troubling story."

"I promise to listen until it's finished."

"Reba and Mando were raised a by a white miner and a Yavapai mother. The Yavapai have lived in this part of Arizona for centuries and, just like in many cases out in the West, they resented it when white miners began to flood into their lands in search of gold and silver. One of those miners was a man named Clayton Parker and he discovered a vein of pure gold up in the Granite Mountains."

"And he would be Mando and Reba's father?"

"Yes," Dolly said. "From what I've heard, Clayton Parker was a wild, crude and dangerous man. I don't know why he married a Yavapai, but he was very hard on his family, forcing them to work his claim while he often came to Prescott to drink and gamble. He seemed to have an endless supply of gold and he was a braggart and bully, generally hated by everyone."

Darby blew a cloud of smoke at the ceiling. "Let me guess. Clayton Parker came to a bad end."

"And sadly, so did his Yavapai wife. Some men to whom he owed a lot of gambling money followed him into the mountains hoping to locate Clayton Parker's secret gold mine. When Clayton refused to talk there was a gun battle. Clayton and his wife were shot to death and their children escaped then hid in the brush in order to save their lives."

"And when you heard about this, you immediately set out to help the Parker children," Darby guessed aloud.

"Of course! They were starving on Granite Mountain and terrified of white men, so I had a deuce of a time getting them to come to Prescott. I kept them hidden for a while but Mando couldn't stand being imprisoned inside, so I asked the stable owner if he would allow the young man to stay and work in exchange for his keep. The owner was very dubious about that but when he saw that Mando was tall and strong and that he'd been working since he was able to walk, he took him on. Reba stayed here to help and keep me company. She's very smart and interesting."

"So why wasn't that a happy ending for Clayton's half-breed children?"

"Two reasons. First, Clayton had cheated so many people in Prescott and had also shot a popular citizen, that he was both feared and hated. But the second reason is that men wanted to know where to find his gold mine."

"But I thought you said they tracked and killed him and his Indian wife at the claim."

"When they cornered Clayton and his family, they thought they had, but the man was cunning, and he would never go directly to his claim. He and his family had a little shack they lived in some undetermined distance from the gold mine. The bunch that killed Clayton and his wife searched in vain for the location of his gold mine but never found it. This, of course, made them furious and for some reason they put the blame on Reba and Mando. They believe that those two are the only ones that can lead them to the gold."

Dolly paused. "You probably noticed my broken windows."

"I did."

"Someone threw rocks and broke them a few nights ago. What they want is for me to force Reba and Mando to reveal where their father's gold mine is so they can collect their debts … with interest."

"Do the pair even know where their father's gold mine is to be found?"

"Of course. They worked the claim along with their parents for years."

Darby thought on that for a few moments. "Then perhaps Mando should just tell them where the gold is and be done with it."

"It's a little more complicated than that," Dolly said slowly. "You see, Mando and Reba Parker are understandably bitter about the murder of their mother."

"Of course, they would be, but …"

"When General George Crook took command of Fort Whipple he dealt very harshly with the Yavapai and some of the other Indian tribes like the Hualapai and Havasupai. They were all driven down to the Apache reservation at San Carlos and a lot of them died. Finally, in small family groups, knowing that they would not survive down in the lower desert country on Apache land, they started stealing away from the reservation and returning here where they were born and raised."

"Like the Cherokee and Navajo."

"Yes," Dolly agreed. "And by the time these local Indians struggled back here from San Carlos, all their best land had been taken by miners and farmers. So, they had no way to return to their old life. They became beggars and almost like slaves just in order to eat and survive."

Dolly took a ragged breath, clearly overcome with sadness. "The truth is that Mando and Reba believe that what gold is left should be mostly used to help the desperately poor Yavapai people."

"I see," Darby said quietly. "Has Reba or Mando given you any idea how much gold might still be at the claim?"

"No, because even they don't know. All they can say is that it is a thin, but pure vein that goes into the mountain and that the mine entrance is very well hidden."

Darby frowned. "That's a noble commitment to help the Yavapai, but it has put you in danger."

"I don't think any of the men who killed their mother and father would kill me. But when I'm in the middle of town shopping I sometimes see rough-looking strangers glaring at me with hatred and I'm sure they are thinking that, if they forced me to talk, I would be able to tell them where to find the secret gold mine."

"Is there a sheriff or marshal who could help?"

"There's a town marshal but he is probably one of the men that cornered and killed Clayton and his Indian wife. I say this because I know he was owed gambling money. Sweetest Treat, our town marshal would be of no assistance whatsoever."

"What a mess!"

"It is," Dolly agreed. "But I know you will find a solution to our troubles."

Darby didn't have a solution but that didn't mean that one could not be found. It was a problem that would take some thinking on and a little time ... or maybe more than a little.

"Dolly, first thing tomorrow we'll find someone to repair those broken front windows."

"Why? They'll just be broken again and again until this issue of secret gold is resolved."

Darby realized that was likely true. Still, he was here at last with Dolly now and he meant to make a stand and set things right. He had seen the shadow of fear and suspicion in Reba's eyes and, also, those of Mando. They did not deserve to live this way and neither did their ragged and displaced people that he had already noticed begging in the Plaza and on the busy streets of Prescott.

CHAPTER 12

When Ruff, Dixie and Houston had finished their dinner, they decided to take a walk down to the stable and make sure everything was fine with their Thoroughbreds.

"I think each of us should take turns and spend the night with our horses sleeping in the barn," Dixie told her brothers. "We can't afford to have them stolen again and a few of the mares are ready to foal."

"I agree," Ruff said. "I'll take tonight."

"I'll take it tomorrow night," Houston said.

"Fine," Dixie said. "I'll take the next."

The brothers stopped in the street and Ruff tipped back his Stetson. "Sister, that half Indian kid, Mando, sleeps in the barn every night. It wouldn't be proper for you spend the night alone in there with him."

"You know me," Dixie said. "I can take care of myself."

"Of course you can," Houston said, "but if we are really going to make a life here, then the last thing we need is bad talk about anyone's behavior. You know how people gossip."

Dixie chewed on that for a moment. "I wouldn't be alone," Dixie countered. "I'll have all our Thoroughbreds."

"You know that isn't our meaning," Houston said. "Mando is about your age and it isn't proper that he stay with you all night."

Dixie looked from one of her brothers to the other and she knew they would not yield on this issue, but it still stuck in her craw to back down. "Well, then Mando will just have to find somewhere else to sleep when it's my turn."

The Ballou brothers didn't like the sound of that but since they had no better idea, they let the discussion drop.

Inside the big stable barn, a lamp glowed, and they saw Mando brushing High Man. The foundation stallion was munching on some grass hay and he looked satisfied to be brushed in a well-made barn.

"He is a fine animal," Mando told them. "But he is old, yes?"

"Yeah," Ruff said, "and the long journey from Tennessee hasn't be easy on any of us these past years, but I expect it has been toughest on High Fire."

"This one," Mando said, gesturing toward High Fire, "he is the son?"

"He is," Dixie answered. "You've got a good eye for horses, Mando."

"I love and trust them ... always. And the mares are in foal. There will be foals coming soon. Four or five, eh?"

"Yes," Dixie said. "They will come soon, and they are *very* important to us."

"Of course."

The Ballou people looked around the interior of the barn which was large and well kept. "Where is the man that owns this?"

"He is a good man but very old," Mando explained. "He comes around once or twice a week walking with a cane. He lets me stay here for nothing."

"I'd say you earn your keep," Dixie offered.

"It is not work for me to care for horses. They are my friends and we understand each other."

Ruff had to smile. "We feel exactly the same way."

Mando finished the brushing. He moved slowly around the horses, talking in a low voice that was meant to sooth and reassure them.

"Mando, have you always been around horses?" Houston asked.

"Yes. Not ones so beautiful like these, but horses are horses, no?"

"They are. Where did you live before you came to live in this barn?" Dixie asked.

Even in the dark they could see the sudden caution in Mando's eyes, the suspicion and wariness. Finally, he said, "I lived in the mountains not so far away."

"What did you do there?"

Mando did not answer but managed a sad smile before he moved out of the lamplight and found himself a place to lie down in the straw. It was clear to the Ballou people that he was done answering questions.

The next morning, Ruff, Dixie and Houston decided to ride over to Fort Whipple and talk to the officials about their horses and the general state of affairs in the Prescott area. If they were serious about buying land to raise racehorses, it would be important to get the Army's take on the future.

"Mando," Ruff said, "we'll be back before dark; we are going to have a look at Fort Whipple."

Mando's gave them a nod and went back into the barn.

"Strange fella," Ruff said.

"He's half Indian and I'm sure that he's had some troubles with Indian-hating whites. Maybe even the Army."

"That stands to reason."

Fort Whipple was a large collection of log buildings including barracks, officers' quarters, mess hall and stables, all surrounding an expansive parade ground. It was near the creek and on slightly higher ground with a good view of the mountains. When the Ballou people arrived, the cavalry was just finishing up a spirited drill that involved about twenty men and horses. Leading the drill was a captain riding a fine bay gelding. When the drill was completed, a bugler blew a call and the men dismounted.

"Excellent work. Company, dismissed!"

The officer rode over to meet his visitors, eyes fixed on their exceptional horses.

"I'm Captain Quaid, and I haven't seen Thoroughbreds since I last visited Kentucky way back in the spring of 1860. You people must hail from Dixie."

"We do," Ruff said. "Tennessee born and raised as were these horses."

"What I wouldn't give to have an animal like that to ride," the captain said wistfully. "Out here we have lots of good horses, many whose lines go all the way back to the Spanish and early mustangs. They're quick, tough and sure-footed, which is what we need in this rough country, but what you people are riding are horses reserved for the gods."

The Ballou riders beamed with pride. Dixie said proudly, "Our father spent his lifetime developing this line of Thoroughbreds. Unfortunately, he is gone and so is the life we enjoyed in the South. But we're hoping to make a new start in this Arizona Territory."

The Captain nodded with understanding. "Yes, the Confederacy was beaten, and its lands stolen by carpetbaggers. But her spirit will never be broken. Still and all, there is much to be said about the opportunities to be found in the great American West."

Quaid studied the surrounding hills and mountains and it was obvious from the expression on his rugged face that he found the views pleasing. "So, what can I do to help you folks today?"

"We've only just arrived in Prescott. We were thinking of perhaps settling here and buying some land for a horse ranch and perhaps even raise a few cattle for our table and to sell."

"This is a fine place to do that," the captain said. "But land with water is not cheap. And with livestock, as you well know, you need plenty of water to raise your own hay for the stock because it's darned expensive to buy."

"If he has the time," Houston said, "we'd like to talk to your commanding officer."

"He's in Tucson and isn't planning to return for a month or so but I'll try to help you. Why don't we go into the officers' building and talk?"

"That'd be fine."

Captain Quaid signaled for several of the soldiers to come take care of the horses. It was clear from their expressions that they were just as impressed as their captain was with the very tall and handsome Thoroughbreds.

Once inside the officers' building, they took seats and wasted no time in small talk. "How much land are you looking for?"

"Depends on the land prices," Houston said. "We lost most everything in the war and so we're not long on cash."

"But you have more Thoroughbreds in Prescott?"

"Our mares are all in foal," Dixie told him. "Same bloodline as we're riding."

Ruff leaned forward in his chair. "Being as how it's obvious that the grass doesn't grow nearly as thick and tall as it did in Tennessee, I figure we'll need a minimum of eight hundred acres of flat land, without it being rocky, *and* a permanent source of water. We'd prefer a river or stream but if the water table is high, shallow wells with good capacity might work."

"Rivers? What are they?" the captain joked. "Out here there isn't much other than the Colorado and that's a long ways off. So, you must look for a good creek or stream and that means you probably want to buy some land on Granite Creek. And it just so happens there is a ranch for sale not two miles from Fort Whipple."

"Any idea how much land or the price?" Houston asked.

"It's in the neighborhood of a thousand acres. Good river bottom land and it has derelict buildings, but the burned down ranch house is almost a total loss."

"How'd they get burnt out?"

"Yavapai Indians were raiding some years ago. Apache, too. Often, they raided together and that's why this fort was built. Now, however, the Indians have all been subjugated and are no longer a threat. Because of that, the people in Washington are talking about making this fort a military hospital or retirement facility for old officers and soldiers who have no family. The climate is very healthful. I expect this fort to be here for many years and that makes the citizens of Prescott happy. We pump quite a bit of money into that town."

Houston frowned. "Captain, do you have any idea of the price of this abandoned ranch?"

"No, but the National Bank of Arizona holds the title and will have set a price. I understand there have been offers made but declined. Because it has good bottom land with a year-around stream it will sell before long. I'll tell you that when it was raided and burned out, an entire family and three of their workers were slaughtered. That being said, not a lot of people want to live there. You know, ghosts and all that."

"We don't believe in ghosts," Dixie said quickly, "but we're sorry about the massacre."

"It was before my arrival, but I hear it was terrible. During the raid, the Indians took the cattle and goats and they roasted the chickens in the fires they used to burn the ranch house. The Army set out after them and tracked them down over near Lynx Creek. Killed a couple dozen of them and rounded the rest up and shipped 'em off to the reservation."

"So, I take it this ranch is deserted?" Houston asked.

"That's right. It was called the River Ranch. I'm told that the family who lived there raised cattle, a lot of chickens and goats and sold all they could provide not only to our supply officer, but also on the Prescott plaza."

"Any fencing still standing?"

"Some," the captain said. "But the place has been abandoned for at least five years."

"If we raised some cattle on the side, would the Army buy our beef?" Dixie asked.

"Why sure, Miss. If you added chickens, we'd buy eggs and we'd buy whatever else you would care to sell, so long as your prices were competitive." The captain steepled his fingers. "We buy our hay from the Long Meadow Ranch and from Johnny Koontz in the upper Williamson Valley. Koontz also raises and breaks teams of horses and we buy them from him for $75.00 a pair."

"We're not in the business of raising wagon horses,

Captain," Ruff explained.

"Oh, I can sure see that! Where are you going to race?"

"Anywhere there's a track and money to be won or lost," Dixie answered.

"Well, people around here love horse races. There's a fella named Charley Young who catches wild mustangs. He works for the Cross-Triangle Ranch north of here. We buy a lot of cavalry horses from Charley. Once they're broke right, they generally prove to be outstanding Army mounts. They are extremely sure-footed, tough and they don't eat a lot of feed."

Dixie, Ruff and Houston had heard enough. They said goodbye to the captain, took a long look at the cavalry horses being cared for in the stable then headed upstream until they came to the old River Ranch.

For the next three hours, they closely inspected the property and the captain had been right in saying that it was in very bad shape. As for the house, only the chimney was still standing. The roof had been set afire, so it had fallen in and the barns and corrals were in serious need of repair. In the main barn there were old campfires and discarded tin cans and whiskey bottles and even a pair of worn-out boots.

"Given its history and condition this place might actually be something we can afford," Ruff said. "The main thing is the land. It's flat and not at all rocky, except down along the creek. If you agree, I think we should ride back to Prescott, find out the asking price. After that, we can figure out if it will work for us."

"Maybe we should look around at other places," Dixie suggested.

"Maybe," Ruff finally agreed with a shrug of his shoulders.

"Hell," Houston said, "if the price is right and we can finally plant our family roots and make a future here, we shouldn't dilly dally. We've spent years on the move, and I can't think of anything we've seen that would work any better for a horse ranch. I'm thinking that in a year...two at the most...we could have a racetrack and I'll bet that it would be popular among the people hereabouts as well as the off-duty soldiers. You two could make a good go of it here with a racetrack and guaranteed honest betting."

"What does *'you two'* mean?" Ruff asked, studying his brother closely.

Houston toed the ground for a moment and finally looked up and said, "It means that I'm going back to Ash Fork to get better acquainted with Peaches."

"What!" Dixie exclaimed.

"You heard me."

Dixie shook her head in bewilderment. "Look, I know she is real pretty."

"No," Houston corrected, "she's flat out beautiful."

"Even so, I don't think Peaches is going to let you sweep her off her feet. I really believe you are way overestimating your charms. Besides, Peaches sure doesn't need a man anymore since she is now a wealthy widow."

"Oh, trust me that she *needs* a man," Houston said, giving them both a wink and a wide salacious grin. "I have a way of reading women and she's already feeling lonesome and unloved."

Dixie was disgusted with her big brother. "You're incorrigible!"

"I'm just a man looking for an easier life than rebuilding this poor old ranch from the ground up."

"So, what happens if it doesn't work out with Peaches?" Dixie asked with exasperation. "Do you expect to just come riding back here and make yourself at home?"

"Sure, you'd take me in. But if I don't connect with Peaches, then I might just head on back to Tennessee to get some payback from those carpetbaggers who took over our magnificent estate."

"Dammit, Houston, that would be plain foolish!" Dixie snapped.

"Well, I'm sorry that you feel that way, but a man has to do what he feels is his calling in life. Now, why don't you two ride on back to Prescott? I'm closer to Ash Fork so I think I'll just mosey on up there and see whatever love and happiness I might find."

Dixie just shook her head. "Come on, Ruff. Let's see a banker and find out if there's a chance we can figure out a way to buy this property and its water rights."

Houston laughed. "If you need some help, one of you might ride on up to Ash Fork and watch me sweet-talk Peaches into giving us a big ranch loan."

"That'll be the day," Ruff snorted, reining his horse around and putting it into a long, swinging gallop with Dixie coming right behind.

She twisted around in the saddle to see Houston mounting High Man and wondered if she would ever see either the old Thoroughbred stallion or her foolish big brother again.

CHAPTER 13

Darby took a nap and then awoke and went outside to find Dolly and Reba working in the garden. He put his derby on and said, "Dixie, Ruff and Houston rode up to see Fort Whipple and might look at some ranches for sale. I think I'll go down to the stable to see how Mando is doing with the Thoroughbred mares."

"We could come along," Dolly offered.

"No, I won't be long and you both seem to be busy and happy doing your gardening. And after I check on Mando, I'm going to pay the marshal a little visit."

"His name is Marshal Richard Judd and you won't like him," Dolly warned. "Furthermore, I'm dead certain that he won't like you if he knows you've moved into my house."

"Did Marshal Judd have romantic ideas about you?"

Dolly snorted with derision. "He had ideas about me, but they sure weren't *romantic.* The man is a pig but he's not to be taken lightly. I've heard that he can be quite vicious."

"Thanks for the warning, my dear."

She stood up with a worried expression. "I'm serious; treat Marshal Judd with extreme caution."

Darby nodded and then headed for the stable barn. On his way he passed several ladies and tipped his derby to them. "Good day," he said with a welcoming smile.

More than a few turned after he'd passed to watch him with more than casual interest.

When he entered the big Plaza Stable the Derby Man immediately sensed tension. "Mando!"

"Mr. Buckingham, please come quick!"

Darby hurried through the dim interior until he came to a stall where he found Mando with one of the Thoroughbred mares. The animal kept swinging its head around toward its belly and then it groaned and collapsed on the fresh straw bedding.

Mando was instantly at the mare's side with soothing hands and words.

"Mando, what ..."

"She is about to give birth," Mando explained. "We need to help her."

"But ... but she's a *horse*. They must know how to deliver on their own."

"Sometimes there is trouble."

"What can I do?" Darby asked, almost wishing he'd gone to the marshal's office first.

"Get some of those empty grain sacks."

Darby found the sacks and grabbed up an armful. He hurried back to the stall and leaned in close.

"She just broke her water," Mando said, watching

the mare as she groaned and strained. Her breath was coming fast, and she kept throwing her head around.

"Will it just pop out?" Darby asked.

"I hope so."

For several minutes they watched the mare struggle. Her legs were flung out and stiff. Her breathing was a mix of agonized grunts and groans. Then, a white, shiny and very wet sack appeared from between her back legs. Moments later, they could see a pair of spindly legs.

"My god!" Darby whispered. "This is amazing!"

As more of the foal slid out, Mando found a pocketknife and slit the placenta and Darby recoiled despite himself.

Mando leaned closer to the mare and reached out to grab the foal's forelegs and pull. The mare's entire body was contracting; she was grunting and straining with all her strength.

"It's coming!" Darby collapsed to his knees. "Shall I help you pull?"

Mando nodded and Darby took hold of a tiny hoof. It was soft, very unlike any hoof he'd ever touched. He slipped his hand up to the ankle and got a good grip.

"Easy," Mando said. "We pull, but not too hard."

"How do you know this?"

"I don't."

Darby and Mando tugged and the legs came out farther, past the knees but then, everything stopped coming out.

"Mando, what's wrong?"

"The head... it should be coming now but it must

be stuck."

"What can we do?"

Mando took a deep, steadying breath. "I will reach in and try to feel the head and maybe it needs a little turning back this way."

Darby didn't have anything to say as he was completely lost about what should be done. *If only the Ballou people were here! They would know what to do.*

Darby watched Mando tear off his shirt and slip his hand into the mare. Mando was breathing every bit as hard as the mare as he probed deeper causing the horse to repeatedly hammer her head on the straw.

"Easy girl," Mando kept whispering. "Easy now. We are going to help you."

"What do you feel?"

Mando was quiet just a moment and then he said. "I feel the nose ... the muzzle. It is turned back."

"Can the head come out that way? Turned back, I mean?"

"I don't think so. I will try to turn it toward the legs."

Mando inched his arm deeper and deeper until it was almost to his shoulder. "I have to get ahold of *something* so that I can ease the head around."

"An ear?"

"I can't find one." He closed his eyes for a second. "I feel the jaw!"

"Can you get ahold of it?"

"I am trying but it is very slippery and ... oh, I think I have it and it is turning!"

Darby wondered if his heart might burst it was pounding so hard and fast. "Easy. Easy!"

Mando strained with all his might and suddenly, he cried, "The head, it came around and I felt it bump over a leg ... it's now between them!"

"Shall I pull harder now?"

"I think so," Mando replied, very slowly extracting his arm and then his hand. "We both pull but slow and steady."

Less than a minute later, the head appeared, then the shoulders and then the foal came sliding out and the mare groaned and stopped struggling. She laid her head down with a long sigh and twisted around as if to see what she had done.

Mando tore the sack away and eased the foal completely out of the mare.

"That was a miracle...but rough. Is the colt still breathing?"

He lifted the foal's head and wiped clear its nostrils. "Yes!"

Darby twisted away and scooted over to be nearer the mare's head. "She's still breathing, too!"

"That's very good."

After that, they both leaned back in the straw feeling exhilarated but exhausted to watch. The mare struggled to her feet and begin to lick her foal.

"It's like she is urging her baby to get up and see the new world," Darby said in a hushed voice. "This is ... *beautiful.*"

"Yes, it is," Mando agreed, grinning from ear to ear.

"What do we do now?"

"We just sit still and watch."

And that's what they did. Sat in the wet, stinking straw and watched as the mare licked and the foal struggled to climb to its feet. In less than a half an hour, it was standing and wobbled over to the mare's teats which were dripping milk.

"He's a hungry little guy," Mando said grinning.

"Very hungry. Is it often that difficult?"

"I don't know," Mando confessed. "I've never done this before."

Mando eased around on the wet straw to sit close to the colt and he patted its wet body. "Mr. Buckingham, we are a good team. You came along just in time. Miss Dixie and her brothers will be very happy."

They sat watching the colt suckling and the mare who let out what almost sounded like a long sigh that Darby was sure was an expression of pure relief.

"Is it really true you never did this before?"

"Not counting dogs, I have seen it happen twice," Mando admitted. "But that was with a goat and a milk cow. Almost always the legs and then the head come out first and when the shoulders appear, the body just slides out quickly."

"Would the mare have died if you hadn't reached inside and turned the head back?"

Mando thought about that carefully and answered, "Maybe. Or maybe she would have finally found a way to push the colt out, but it would have been born dead."

"I see."

Darby walked back outside where he knew there

was a water trough. He used one of the empty grain sacks to clean himself up as best he could and then he went back inside with a damp sack and pitched it to Mando who washed and put his shirt back on. Darby felt powerfully energized and very pleased with himself.

"I will never forget this. I might even write about it someday."

"Pretty messy," Mando said, looking down at his own soiled clothing.

"Messy, but magnificent," Darby said to the young man as he pulled on his shirt and then coat. "Now, I'm off to pay a visit to the marshal."

Mando's smile melted.

"It'll be alright."

Mando followed him outside. "Don't push that marshal," he warned.

"I'm not afraid of any man."

"I mean, don't get locked up in case one of the other mares needs us."

Darby managed a nod. His pants were a mess and he felt physically spent so he found a fresh cigar and lit it. He was really looking forward to a glass of whiskey.

"I'll be back soon."

Marshal Richard Judd was not a big man. He was maybe five feet eight inches and weighed about 160 pounds. But what he lacked for in size he made up in arrogance and nastiness. The moment Darby entered his cluttered little pig sty of an office, Judd dropped his boots from his desk, stood up, placed his hands on his hips and said, "I *know* who you are."

"Congratulations," Darby said, tightly. "I come to ask why in the hell you are not arresting whomever it is that is harassing Miss Beavers and Miss Parker?"

"You smell like shit," Judd said, wrinkling his nose. "What have you been doing, rutting with pigs?"

It took everything Darby had not to hurl himself across the room, grab the marshal by the throat and shake him like a terrier would a rat.

"Do you really know who you are talking to?"

"I'm talking to an eastern dude who stinks," Marshal Judd hissed.

"If you are one of the ones that are giving Dolly and those two Parker kids trouble, I'm going to come down on you like a ton of rocks."

Judd bristled. "If you come after me, I'll see that you wind up either dead or in the Yuma Territorial Penitentiary. And let me tell you, not many men can survive there and you sure as hell wouldn't be one of them."

"I've broken far better men than you both in and out of the ring," Darby said. "I was warned you were worthless and would do nothing to help Miss Beavers and Clayton Parker's kids. And I understand no arrests were made after men came to a remote shack in the mountains gunned down both Clayton Parker and his wife."

"I seen that Parker squaw and she wasn't bad on the eyes. Maybe they shouldn't have killed her right away." He winked and leered. "Know what I mean?"

Darby knew he was either going to hurt this man badly or he had to leave. And because Dolly and the

Parker kids needed him close, he chose to leave.

"Mister, like I said, you're stickin' your nose into something that is going to get you either killed or sent to prison," Judd warned. "I'm looking forward to see which that is going to be."

Darby stopped at the door and turned back to glare at the miserable little peacock. "I'm going to make sure you are broken," he promised in a quiet voice. "It's going to happen one way or the other."

"Ha! Dolly told me how rich and famous you are, but in Prescott you're just a stinking polecat with a big mouth and a funny hat!"

Darby slammed the door so hard the building shook. He marched down the street along the plaza past the courthouse and came upon a gun shop. Pushing inside with a murderous frame of mind, he minced very few words in letting the owner know that he was interested in buying a double-barred shotgun ... and shells.

The owner was trying to far stand back from his counter and Darby realized that it was because of his own foul stench. His trousers were still soaked in blood and slimy fluids from the equine birth and he would have to burn his suit and even his custom-made shoes.

No matter. He had plenty of money. "Mister, where is the nearest haberdashery or tailor?"

The man gave him clear directions. "No offense, Sir, but that suit you're wearin' smells like skunk squirt mixed with pig shit."

Darby paid the tab, shot the man a murderous glance and headed outside in a huff. But as he passed on by the barn where Mando would be inside working with the newborn colt and watching over the other mares, Darby relaxed.

He had done something pretty special today, and he had formed a bond with a half-breed kid whose life was in real danger. If Darby had had a son, he would have liked him to be a lot like Mando.

Darby slowed his pace and allowed himself a broad smile. All in all, and despite his seething antipathy for the town marshal, it had been a thrilling and remarkable day.

CHAPTER 14

Dixie and Ruff cantered into town and headed straight for the Plaza Stable.

"Mando!" Dixie called.

"I'm back here in a stall," the young man yelled from the barn's dim interior.

Moments later Dixie and Ruff were standing around the handsome colt and its mother with big smiles on their faces.

"Did the little fella come out easy?" Dixie asked.

"A problem, not bad." Mando told them about the colt's head being turned back and how he had seen no other course but to reach in and try to rotate it.

"Where did you learn that?" Ruff asked.

"My mother and her people told me about such things."

"And Mr. Buckingham, what was he doing?"

"He is very strong. We worked well together."

Ruff and Dixie grinned. "Well, you two deserve a lot of credit. This colt looks to me like he will become the spitting image of High Man. I think he might even one day become a great racehorse and sire."

"I hope so," Mando said. "He had a tough start, so he deserves greatness."

Dixie laughed and said, "We can't begin to repay you, Mando. We will be forever be grateful and will think of something."

"It is I who am most grateful. And I think Mr. Buckingham was grateful as well although he will need to buy another new suit."

"No doubt," Ruff said. "Thank you both so much. And I'm glad it's a colt and not a filly. High Man is getting old and High Fire will be ready for some assistance in three or four years."

Dixie and Ruff unsaddled their horses and told Mando that their older brother had ridden back to Ash Fork. They didn't say why and Mando didn't ask. Instead, he said, "Mr. Buckingham, he went to see Marshal Judd. I asked him to be very careful with that man. He is dangerous."

"Well, we'd better see about that and we need to talk to the bank about a ranch we found, Mando."

"Which ranch is that?"

"It's called the River Ranch and it …"

Mando stiffened. "You should not consider that place!"

"Why?"

"It is haunted by Yavapai ghosts."

"We don't believe in ghosts. And if the price is right, it would work out just fine for our new Arizona horse ranch."

Mando did not look at all convinced. He turned away and Ruff added, "After what we've learned just now concerning your love and talent for horses, maybe you would like to come and work for us and get out of Prescott. I understand that you have been threatened. Being a ways out of town would be safer and we'd be there to help protect you from anyone with bad intentions."

"If you buy the ghost ranch, I will think about it. But I do not want to go far from my sister. Reba has also been threatened."

"Maybe we can find a way to take care of that problem," Dixie suggested throwing a glance at her brother who gave her a quick nod. "Can she cook and ride a horse?"

"She is a good cook and hunter," Mando said. "She can shoot rabbits on the run but is not so good with horses."

"That can be learned," Dixie said. "We'd teach both of you everything we have learned from our father and Cherokee mother."

Mando's eyes widened. "You are also part *Indian?*"

"Yes," Ruff said. "The Ballou are all half-breeds the same as you and Reba. Just different tribes. Cherokee and Yavapai."

Mando smiled to learn this news. "When I looked at you three, I felt that maybe you had some good Indian blood in your veins. Who are these Cherokee people you speak of?"

"They live on the other side of this country. They were hill people who had their own written language and even had plantations before everything was taken away from them."

"Like with my people," Mando said quietly. "They

had to walk down into the desert and live among the Apache. They were not wanted at San Carlos and many died."

"Many Cherokee died as well in Oklahoma."

They were all quiet for a moment not knowing what else could be said. So Dixie broke the awkward silence. "Ruff, let's go see the banker and find out if there is any way to buy that land and borrow enough money to start fixing it up as a horse ranch. Should we rename it the Ghost Ranch... that's what Mando just called it?"

"I like the River Ranch name better, but it doesn't matter all that much to me. We can ask Houston which he prefers and take a vote."

Dixie nodded because she thought that was a fine solution. To her way of thinking, there were a lot of River Ranches all over the country, but this name was unique and so despite Ruff's reservations, she preferred Ghost Ranch. After all, there were likely as many good ghosts as well as bad living there among the ashes.

On the southeast corner of Gurley and Cortez Streets stood the National Bank of Arizona and they were immediately directed to the manager, Robert Tillman.

"So, you've come all the way from Tennessee looking for a place to build a Thoroughbred horse ranch?" he asked after he'd heard their story.

"That's right," Dixie said. "But we don't have a lot of cash. That's why we're looking at a run-down place with a bad history called the River Ranch."

"Ah, nice land that!" the banker said effusively.

"And you can't find better grassland or water."

"The ranch house has been burned down to the stone foundation."

"Rock walls and chimney just need to be added on to," the banker said brightly. "Barn, corrals and other outbuildings are still standing."

"Fencing is shot," Ruff commented, "and the place has a very bad image given the circumstances of the massacre."

Tillman drummed his manicured fingers on his desk and leaned back in his office chair. He studied the young pair. "Do you mind me asking exactly why you came all the way out here to the Arizona Territory? I mean, Tennessee must have lots of water and tall grass. Probably dozens of great Thoroughbred stables and ranches. But out here … well, it's fine country, but rough and raw."

"We like the views," Dixie answered, "and we think this territory has a bright future."

Tillman managed a tolerant smile. "I appreciate your youthful optimism and we certainly could use you both working in the territorial state house. However, we lost our capital standing for ten years and we've just gotten it back from Yuma. Now, the folks in Tucson want it and there's a lot more in Phoenix that are clamoring for the capital to be established in their fast-growing city."

"What are you really tryin' to tell us?" Ruff asked.

"I'm saying that, if you're counting on Prescott to always be the territorial capital, you're making a bad bet. The mines hereabouts have nearly played out. More copper and silver are being pulled out of the

Jerome mines and one down in Wickenburg called the Vulture Mine."

Dixie and Ruff sat quietly for a few minutes. Finally, Dixie asked the question that was on both her and her brother's mind. "Mr. Tillman, we understand your bank owns the River Ranch. And we were told by the captain out at the fort that it is for sale. So, if that is all true, why on earth are you *downplaying* the River Ranch property and Prescott?"

The banker looked away for a moment, then back at Dixie and Ruff. "In regard to the ranch, I think we have a solid offer coming in very soon. One that I doubt you could match. I'm just trying to save us all a lot of wasted time."

"What's the asking price?" Ruff demanded.

"Three thousand dollars for one thousand acres, a good water well that just needs cleaning out and all those outbuildings and what's left of the house. The fencing alone is worth hundreds of dollars."

"Three thousand." Dixie shook her head and let out a sigh. "Well, Brother, I think we need to have a long talk and time to think this thing out."

"Why?" Ruff asked. "We don't have nearly that much cash."

Dixie winked. "We don't, but maybe someone else does."

Ruff nodded as he read his sister's mind. Coming to his feet he extended his hand to the banker and said, "First one with the money gets the ranch?"

"That's right. We don't deal in talk. Talk is cheap but money wins the day."

"Fair enough, Mr. Tillman." Ruff looked at his

sister and then they left the bank.

Once outside, they strolled across the plaza and saw the new capital building and how it was being expanded, and there were a number of other buildings under construction.

"Dixie, I know you're thinking of asking Darby Buckingham for a loan."

"Or a part interest in what will become a great Arizona horse ranch."

"He hardly knows horses and told me that he likes them but can't ride worth a damn."

"He loves the West and he loves Miss Beavers," Dixie countered. "And if she is determined to remain in this part of the territory, well, maybe he would consider doing that as well. And we've already been thinking about asking Mando to help us out and his younger sister would be a fine addition. While I'm working with the new foals and helping you with the horses, she and her brother could be chopping wood, cooking and doing a hundred things that neither of us like nor are good at doing."

Ruff barked a laugh. "Dixie, you seem to have this all figured out."

"I come to conclusions faster than you do. You've always told me so and it's true."

"So what now?" Ruff asked.

"We talk to Mr. Buckingham and to Miss Beavers. Soon enough, we'll know if we're going to own the Ghost Ranch."

"River Ranch," Ruff corrected.

Dixie allowed herself a small smile. "We'll just see about that if we can buy the place."

CHAPTER 15

As he neared the town of Ash Fork, Houston Ballou figured he would go to a little extra trouble and expense before calling on the very recently widowed Peaches Patterson. He put High Man up at the stable and the owner asked, "How long you gonna be here?"

"I have no idea," Houston replied.

He paid the stableman for one night's keep of High Man, but he was thinking that if he and Peaches hit it off well, then he'd be here quite a bit longer. He headed up the street, knocking dust off his pants and, on the way to the barber's shop, he passed the big mercantile that Peaches had inherited from her dead husband. He peered inside but instead of seeing the lovely Peaches there was a tall young man at the counter.

Houston waved and smiled, and the man waved and smiled back.

"Come on in, Mister! You look like you could use some new clothes and boots."

Houston hesitated and then stepped inside.

"Lookin' for anything special I can help you with?"

Houston shook his head and moseyed down the aisles looking at everything. When he came to the men's clothing section, he carefully considered the shirts and chose the most expensive one available in his size. He found a pair of pants and then a new hat to replace his old, battered one that he'd worn since leaving Tennessee. And finally, he tried on several pairs of boots and found a nice pair of black shiny ones that he figured he could break in to fit comfortably.

Back at the counter, Houston place all his intended purchases on the counter.

"My oh my," the tall young man said with a broad smile, "you sure know how to shop for the best." He turned and pulled a beautiful blue silk bandana off a rack and slid it through his slender fingers. "This one would look fantastic with that hat and shirt. Only two dollars and it's imported from the Orient."

Houston took the bandana and also ran it through his fingers. "Mighty nice. I'll take it."

The total bill came for thirty-six dollars, but Houston figured it was worth that at twice the price. When he had his purchases wrapped up, he asked where he could get a bath, shave and haircut and the handsome clerk pointed the way just down the street.

Houston reached for his money clip.

"Once you get bathed, shaved and your hair cut, when you put on this new outfit and you're definitely going to be the handsomest man in Ash Fork."

"Except for maybe you," Houston said, feeling

good about things. "By the way, where is Peaches … I mean Miss Patterson?"

"She's with some of the leading ladies of the town. They're planning on a church auction to raise money for those less fortunate than ourselves."

"That's kind of her," Houston said. "When is this auction?"

"Tonight. I expect everyone that is anyone in Ash Fork will be there. Say, you ought to come too!"

The offer seemed so genuine and well intentioned that Houston nodded his head. "I believe I just might."

"Well, it's just up the street at the Methodist Church and it starts at seven. Be a lot of people there. Tickets are three dollars."

"*Three* dollars?"

"Yep. And every penny of it in addition to the auction proceeds goes to the charity fund. I got tickets to sell right here. You can buy as many as you want … I mean if you have someone special to bring."

Quick as anything, the tickets were on the counter and by the way the young man spoke, it left no doubt that he thought Houston was a high roller with a lady friend.

"One ticket will be enough," Houston said, grabbing up his things before he was asked to spend even more money. "By the way, what's your name?"

"I'm Peter Patterson."

Houston was so stunned that he almost dropped his packages.

"I'm the son of Jefferson Patterson who died recently of a gunshot wound right in front of this store."

Houston managed to say, "I didn't know Patterson even had a son."

"When I heard my father was shot dead, I was living down in Phoenix. Me and my father weren't close. He was very hard on my mother and divorced her many years ago. In fact, I hardly knew him, but he was my father and of course I had to come and take things over here in Ash Fork."

"What about Mrs. Patterson?"

"Peaches?"

"Yeah." Houston was trying not to appear angry or upset, but this was *terrible* news.

Peter winked. "Well, we could have had a real difficult situation … legal wise, you know … but I think we're going to be able to avoid all of that nastiness."

Houston placed the packages down and leaned forward on the counter for support.

"How, exactly?"

"We're about the same age and took to each other right off the mark. We quickly realized it was better to work together and avoid all the legal expenses."

"So you …"

"We came to an agreement and now we're fixin' to be married!" Peter said, looking as happy as a flea in a doghouse.

Houston groaned.

"Sir, are you alright?"

Tall and handsome young Peter hurried around the counter and took Houston's arm. "Perhaps you should just sit down for a few minutes. Or I could send someone for a doctor, only he isn't a *real* doctor but ..."

"I need a big drink," Houston whispered.

"There's a saloon just three doors down and you do look a little pale. Now that you've paid for that ticket and your purchases you can just leave them here until you've had that drink and have gotten spruced up."

All of Houston's happy designs for Peaches now were gone like smoke in the wind. If she was engaged to this young dandy, he might as well climb back on his horse, tuck his tail between his legs and ride back to Prescott.

He had two straight whiskies in the Wild Hog Saloon and sat brooding at a back table, trying to decide what to do next. If he just left Ash Fork and gave up the idea of winning over Miss Peaches, he'd feel like a quitter. And after all, young Peter Patterson was handsome but hardly more than a dandy. He'd never fought in a war or broke horses and killed men in self-defense. Probably never even been in a knife fight or a vicious brawl.

Instead of ordering a bottle of whiskey for the long ride back to Prescott, Houston came to his feet, squared his shoulders and headed off to get a bath, shave and haircut. He had paid three damn dollars for a ticket to go to the church social and in his new clothes, he knew he'd cut quite a handsome and dashing figure for all the women ... including the beautiful Peaches.

The Ballou way was not to quit when it seemed the game was lost ... it was to fight and win the day!

The church social was in a large hall and it was crowded when Houston arrived, shaved and bathed, in his new clothes and wearing his fine hat and boots.

There were two fiddlers somewhere in the back of the hall, but you couldn't see them because they were sitting down. Their music was sedate and over on the right side of the hall was a big punch bowl where a lot of the younger men were clustered. Houston figured the punch would be without any *punch* but that the men would be fortifying it when they thought no church woman was watching. Along the other side of the room was a long table covered with cakes, pies and other desserts that Houston figured would be the auction items.

Peaches Patterson was dressed in a beautiful yellow satin gown and her hair was done up on top of her head with a green ribbon. She looked magnificent ... far nicer than she had when she'd been hitched to her old husband. And hovering over Peaches was young Peter Patterson, well dressed and grinning like a possum eating a yellow jacket.

Houston caught Peaches' eye and he nodded with a bold wink. He was sure that Peaches blushed slightly, although she kept up a conversation with some lady that was almost fat enough to join a sideshow.

Then Houston turned his back on Peaches and got himself some punch. It was pretty much watered down, but he remembered this was an event to raise money for the poor.

After a few minutes, the two fiddlers jumped out of their seats and came over to the punch bowl. They were short, skinny guys with buck teeth that stuck out so far they could have eaten popcorn out of a jug. Houston was sure they were twins.

"Evenin'," one said, pulling out a bottle and leaning in close to fill half his cup and that of his brother with what was probably mountain moonshine. "Want a little white lightnin'?"

"Why not?" Houston replied.

The fiddlers gulped down their punch and got to fiddling lively tunes that made the crowd smile and start dancing. Houston found himself being corralled and then grabbed by a short brunette that was both pretty and frisky.

"Hey, handsome, let's do some dancin'!" she yelled, dragging him out in the middle of the room.

Houston liked to dance and he was good at it. He began high-stepping, prancing and swinging the brunette around. They were both laughing and having a wonderful time and when the song was over, they carried right on with dancing to the next song.

"Say, mister," she yelled into his face, "I saw you and your brother with them tall horses when you were through town not so long ago. Your little sister and the big dude shot that asshole, Mr. Patterson. Killed him deader than a can of corned beef!"

"Yes, they did."

"Hallelujah! Did this town a big favor!"

"Well, I'm glad there are no hard feelings," Houston said, a little bit surprised at her enthusiasm.

"None at all! Not even with that skinny son come up from Phoenix like a vulture to a carcass. I never thought I'd get the chance to get acquainted, but here we are! Dancin' and romancin'!"

Houston was thinking this was turning out just fine. In his experience, nothing made a man look more attractive to a woman than having other women pay him a lot of attention.

"What's your name, Miss!"

"Lula May!" she called back to him as he whirled her around and around.

And so they danced three dances until what Houston expected to happen, surely did happen. Peaches who had been dancing with Peter and wearing a serious look on her pretty face, accidently bumped Lula May hard enough to knock her sprawling on the floor.

Houston bent and helped her to her feet. Lula May looked ready to fight.

"Oh, I'm so sorry!"

Lula May was furious. "You did that on purpose, didn't you, Peaches!"

"Why, why ever would I do such a thing?" she said, taking Houston's arm and finishing the dance.

Lula May glared at them and when Houston caught a look at Peter Patterson, he appeared mad enough to kick his own dog.

When the fiddlers stopped to rest and refill their glasses, Houston quickly ushered Peaches out of a side door into the church yard. They were both a little winded and their breath came out in quick, cold clouds. Then, before Peaches could say a word, Houston gathered her in his arms and kissed her passionately.

Peaches threw her own arms around his neck and

returned the passion. They would have kissed even more but Peter suddenly appeared.

"Well," he said, voice dripping with sarcasm, "I can see that you two must have been *well* acquainted before I arrived in Ash Fork."

"Yeah," Houston said, almost gloating, "but not quite well enough."

Peter Patterson gave him a look that would kill, but Houston didn't care. The young dandy sure wasn't going to do anything physically about the situation, so Houston just smiled and then ignored him.

"Well," Peaches said, when the young man was gone, "you just might have cost me a small fortune."

"Yeah," Houston said happily, "I met him in your store, and he told me that you were about to tie the knot. I guess I just messed those plans up."

"No, I don't think so," Peaches said, pulling away. "My lawyer says that there was a will and it left something to Peter ... but even so I have a strong claim to the mercantile and all my late husband's assets."

"So how is that going to work out when you and me get married and go to live in Prescott?"

"It ain't," Peaches said flatly. "Because I'm not marrying you and I'm not moving to Prescott ... at least not until all the Patterson financial issues are settled in my favor."

Houston reached around and attempted to caress her bottom, but the big dress made that impossible. "Why don't you and me go where you sleep and then we can discuss our future together in private?"

She threw her head back at the moon and laughed. "Why Houston, you bold, bad rascal! I do believe you have lechery on your mind."

"Definitely."

Peaches studied his handsome face for a moment, then slowly shook her head. "I'm not going to let myself fall in love with you."

"Nobody says we have to *fall in love* at first."

He tried to pull her in tight, but she broke free and said, "You are pure woman poison! I'm going back inside and be a lady again. That's what's expected of me by all the church women."

"What a shame," he said, meaning it. "Are you actually going to marry that milk toast instead of a real *man?"*

"I've already been married to a man and he was a monster. I think I might like the taste of milk toast."

"You have no idea of the mistake you are making," Houston said, meaning every word of it.

"I'm sure you're right. Why don't you go back in with me and take up with Lula May again? Then tomorrow, when you ride back to Prescott, Lula May can tell me exactly how much of a man I passed up on for a time."

"If that's the way you really want it, Peaches."

"I'm afraid that it is," she said, heading back into the hall.

Houston expelled a deep sigh of regret then he entered the hall and saw Lula May looking at him a little hurt and at the same time a little hopeful. He gave her his best winning smile and headed across the dance floor. Two or three more dances and then they'd be gone, and he would almost have forgotten all about Peaches.

Early the next morning Houston left Lula May sleeping. When he stepped outside, the air was cold and invigorating and he needed some powerful invigorating after the night they'd shared. Houston yawned, scratched and studied the first rays of sunrise trying to poke through some clouds way off to the east ... maybe all the way to Tennessee. It was time to go find his brother and sister and then see what needed to be done in Prescott.

He buttoned up his new shirt and pants, heard the squeak of protesting leather from his new boots and fixed his gun on his hip and his Bowie knife under his belt. His hat felt a little tight this morning and he thought that might be because he'd had quite a bit to drink after the church social. But a good ride on a great horse like High Man would clear his mind and raise his spirits.

Sure, he'd failed to win Peaches and the chance to use some of her money to help buy the Ballou family a new ranch ... but a man didn't always easily win in life and he'd had a fine time in Ash Fork. Perhaps, if he did decide to head on back to Tennessee, he would ride through this town again and see if Peaches had tossed the young man aside or married him for money and then buried him.

Houston was sure something like that would happen and he almost felt sorry for Peter Patterson.

He trudged down the deserted street and came to the barn. When he threw open the big barn door it was dark inside and he scowled. Now how was he going to find his horse and saddle the tall

Thoroughbred in the dark?

"Freeze," a cold voice told him on his right.

"One move and you're dead," said another on his left.

Houston was suddenly was wide awake. "Take it easy, fellas. And if you're after money, I already spent it all yesterday on a new outfit and whiskey."

"We're after a *reward,"* the man on the right hissed. "Five hundred dollars compliments of the Confederacy."

"The Confederacy is *dead,"* Houston reminded them quietly.

"And so are you about to be."

Houston whirled in the semi-darkness and threw out an arm. It batted the man on the right full in the face breaking his nose and he yelled and staggered. Tearing out his Bowie knife, Houston heard the man on his left curse and then fire wildly and at near point-blank range in panic. Gunpowder seared Houston's fist and the bullet meant for him missed and struck the bounty hunter Houston had just backhanded. Houston ducked and plunged his knife into the second man's belly, then he heaved his blade upward tearing through guts.

In just a few seconds, the fight was over. Houston stepped outside and took a deep, steadying breath of the cold morning air. He turned to watch the dying pair of Southern bounty hunters crab around in the dirt and when they stopped moving, he rifled their pockets taking just a few dollars in cash and some other things he figured he'd probably discard on his ride back to Prescott. But one thing he would not discard was the neatly folded *Confederate Wanted Poster* with sketches naming him and Ruff Ballou, listing them as traitors, murderers and thieves. And yes, the reward was for five hundred dollars *each.*

"It just wasn't worth it, was it?" Houston said to the dead bounty hunters as he slipped the reward poster into his new shirt's pocket. "Not near enough worth it to come all the way from Tennessee to die in Ash Fork, Arizona."

But of course, he got no answer.

Houston was more than ready to leave Ash Fork. He'd come with the idea of maybe falling in love and getting something from Peaches ... hell, maybe everything. That hadn't worked out as planned but he'd had himself quite a time, and now he knew for sure that the Confederacy... whatever form it had taken...was not in a forgiving frame of mind.

They wanted him and Ruff dead and the reward was big enough to see that it happened. *Well,* Houston thought as he wiped his blade clean on one of the dead men's shirts and hurried inside to saddle and ride, *at least they don't have a reward on Dixie.*

It was sundown when an exhausted Houston Ballou rode High Man into the Prescott stable barn. He was holding his reins in his left hand because he had some painful gunpowder burns on his right.

"Mr. Ballou, you look like you need some rest and so does your horse!"

"Yeah, it was an eventful trip," he agreed, handing over his reins. "Mando, just point me to a soft pile of straw and let me sleep late into tomorrow morning."

Mando led a wobbly-legged Houston inside. He laid Houston down on a pile of clean straw and gave him cornbread and cool water.

"You're a good kid," Houston muttered. "Did my brother and sister figure out a way to buy that River Ranch?"

"I don't know. They went to the bank, but I haven't heard."

"Well, I'm afraid I'm not goin' to be of help in that matter."

Houston fell asleep almost instantly.

Mando went out and unsaddled High Man and then took care of the fine Thoroughbred. He stroked the animal's neck, led it to the water trough where it drank and drank. He rubbed the old stallion down and brushed him vigorously by lamplight then grained and put him in a stall.

"You were very thirsty. Hungry too. I will brush you again tomorrow morning so that you can impress your new son!"

High Man nuzzled Mando and nickered softly with weary approval.

CHAPTER 16

On a pleasantly warm afternoon, Darby Buckingham and Dolly Beavers strolled arm in arm around the expansive Prescott Town Plaza observing with interest all the construction that was underway. In addition to enlarging the Territorial Capitol Building, there was new construction on the impressive Yavapai County Courthouse and its additional legislative offices. Dozens of trees had been planted all over the plaza giving the promise of fine shade in the warmest days of summer. And surrounding the plaza, commercial buildings were going up so fast that Gurley, Cortez, Union and Montezuma Streets were crowded with people and wagons loaded with materials.

Among the many new business there was the Diana Saloon owned by a prosperous and colorful Englishman known as 'Uncle Joe' Crane. Nearby was the Prescott National Bank, Hotel Burke, as well as the new Pioneer Drug Store.

Just a few days earlier the *Arizona Miner*

newspaper had carried the humorous but important announcement that:

Dr. Kendall, at the Pioneer Drug Store, recently received three thousand pounds of goods and is now prepared to kill or cure on short notice!

There was also the Arizona Brewery and the well-stocked Prescott Market. The town's new postmaster, Theodore Otis, had opened a jewelry store that Darby had visited and spent some time inside only yesterday.

"This place is really shaping up to be special," Dolly said. "And I love my little house and gardens."

"Of course you do."

"Darby, I have something serious on my mind that I need to talk to you about."

"And that is?"

"It's about Reba. She has been a wonderful friend and companion while I was waiting for you to return and we've become very close. I admire that girl and her brother. They came from a hard existence and lost their beloved mother who was shot down before their eyes. When they escaped into the timber and brush, they were helped out by an old Yavapai Indian named Ida-heh. But he couldn't feed them, so he brought them into Prescott and I just happened to see the three of them wandering around town looking for someone to help them out."

"And, of course, you *had* to help them."

"Yes. The three of them were dressed in rags and I felt so sorry I invited them into my house for a big meal then bought them decent clothes at the mercantile. I took Mando to the livery and talked the owner into giving him a place to live and work and I took Reba home with me."

"You have a very kind and generous spirit, Dolly. It's one of the things that I love most about you."

She poked him playfully in the ribs. "Oh, you love a lot of other things about me that I won't embarrass you by mentioning."

Darby rolled his eyes and looked away for a moment, fearing he was blushing.

"But the truth is," Dolly said, getting serious again, "I am saddened that I am past the time when I can have children."

"I didn't know that you wanted them."

"I do ... or did. I would have loved having children with you."

In truth, Darby had never wanted kids and actually disliked most of them. Still, not wanting to hurt Dolly's feelings, he tried to look sad and mumbled, "That would have been very nice ... I suppose."

"Reba is smart. When I told her about you being a famous dime novelist, she immediately wanted to see all your books, most of which I have in my library. And then she begged me to read your wonderful stories out loud and, finally, she asked if I thought it was possible that I could teach *her* to read and write."

"That is impressive."

"She's an impressive young woman. I'm teaching her now and she's learning fast. She's even asking me if she could one day write dime novels and become famous."

Darby clapped his thick hands and laughed. "Well, I don't think western dime novels would be her true calling, but she could write about the Yavapai and her amazing life story."

"And serious fiction, too."

"Yes, of course."

"Oh, I'm so happy you understand!"

"Dolly, am I missing something here? What is there to understand?"

Dolly took his hand. "After meeting you, Reba asked me if she could be our daughter."

Darby was caught off guard and it took him a moment to recover. "Do you want her as your daughter?"

"Very much." She looked straight into Darby's eyes. "And I want you to consider her to be your daughter and Mando, our son."

The request was so unexpected that it took Darby a few moments to form a reply, "That's a big request, my dear."

"It is and I didn't know how to even broach the subject, but that's what has been bothering me and what I wanted to say all morning."

"That's certainly understandable."

Darby clasped his hands behind his back. He walked a couple of tight circles around Dolly then stopped and studied his love. "All right, I'll do it!"

"Are you absolutely certain?"

"Yes."

"You must be seriously committed to fatherhood or those two young people would sense it immediately and then likely run away."

He dug a cigar out of his pocket and lit it. He noted that his fingers were trembling ever so slightly.

"Dolly, you've just asked me to agree to something that will dramatically change our lives. And it will also place us in certain danger, because those two know where their late father's gold mine is hidden. So, we not only have to nurture and provide for them, we have to protect them."

"We can do that," Dolly said forcibly. "If I had any doubts, I wouldn't even consider having this conversation. But think of all the good it would do! Not only for them, but for *us.* We would have a family and as the years go by our lives would also be enriched beyond measure."

Darby blew a cloud of smoke into the air and found himself nodding. "You're right. We'll commit to making them a loving home."

Dolly's big blue eyes filled with tears that ran freely down her rosy cheeks. "I *knew* you would agree to be a father!"

He couldn't help but smile. "A *father.* Now that is something I never expected to be."

Dolly gave him a big hug and kissed him in front of everyone and then she took his arm and they continued their little morning stroll around the plaza.

"I understand that plans are already in the works for the Prescott and Arizona Central Railway to be built connecting us with both the transcontinental railroad up in Ash Fork and a short line down to Phoenix. When that happens, it will prove to be a tremendous economic boost to this town."

"Maybe we ought to buy some investment properties here. Do you think that would be a wise thing to do?"

"Perhaps. But first we need to talk about a horse ranch and some other very important things."

"Darby, you've been lost in your own thoughts all morning. Are you working out something in your Santa Fe novel?"

"No."

"Then exactly what are you so concerned about?"

Darby led Dolly Beavers over to a bench and they sat still for a moment before he began to speak. "My darling, we have loved each other for years. We've had great adventures all over the American West. You've been brave and always in good spirits no matter how difficult, or even dangerous, the circumstances."

"Thank you."

"When I was in New Mexico and I received your letter saying that you were in desperate need of help and asking me to come quickly, I was immediately sick with worry. That's why I hired an idiot stagecoach driver and told him to get me to Prescott as fast as possible."

"He almost got you killed in that wreck."

"Yes, he did. But I got here and I was ... well, to be honest, relieved that you were not terminally ill with a cancer or some other terrible disease."

Dolly's expression grew serious. "The trouble we are having about Reba and Mando's secret gold mine is quite serious."

"I know. I know. But I think I have a solution."

Dolly squeezed his arm. "Then let's hear it."

"I want to marry you," Darby blurted. "For me, Reba and Mando, I want you to finally become Mrs. Dolly Buckingham."

Dolly's big blue eyes widened and filled with fresh tears. "Oh, my darling, I am so joyful I think I might burst!"

"Then you'll marry me?"

"Of course!"

Dolly threw her arms around Darby, crushed his neck and kissed him with unrestrained passion. "I am the happiest woman in the world!"

Darby rarely blushed, but now he did. "Then it's settled. We'll visit the jewelry store and I'll show you the engagement ring I picked out. But if it is not to your liking ..."

"Darling, don't you know that I would wear a ring of stinging nettles if it meant we were man and wife?"

Darby was as happy as he'd been in a long, long time, although as a lifetime bachelor he was somewhat overwhelmed by the thought of being both a husband *and* a father. He managed to extract himself from Dolly's arms because he had another serious matter that needed to be discussed and settled.

"I want to invest in the Ballou horse ranch and build us a large house on the property. We would have privacy, and I think sitting on a fine porch and staring off at Thumb Butte and the Thoroughbreds racing around in a huge pasture would be a wonderful way to live. And I could write without the constant interruptions that occur in cities and even small towns like Prescott."

"I have always wanted to own goats," Dolly confessed, "and big, shaggy dogs and chickens and..."

"Whoa!" Darby chuckled. "Let's take it a little slower. Do you agree to live outside of town and side by side with the Ballou family?"

"Of course. And Reba and Mando can live with us?"

"Certainly."

"Then it is settled!" Dolly cried. "We'll get married, build a little ranch house and have animals and Reba and Mando ... and watch Thumb Butte in all seasons and those beautiful Thoroughbred horses."

"I think that would be just fine except for the *little house* part. I want a big, rambling ranch house," Darby said, extending his arms wide. "Let's vow to make that our dream come true."

The evening Ruff and Dixie arrived for dinner at Dolly's house on Union Street. Dolly had gotten her two front windows repaired and, with Reba Parker's help, had prepared a big fried chicken dinner with mashed potatoes, fresh tomatoes and beans from the garden with apple pie for dessert.

"It's nice to sit down together like a family," Ruff said, raising his glass. "Let's have a toast to what good things might lie ahead for us in this new Arizona Territory."

Dolly raised her glass. "We might as well make our announcement right now ... Darby and I are getting married in a few days."

Ruff and Dixie shouted, and Reba clapped her hands.

There was a torrent of questions, but Darby made it clear that the details were not yet settled, but it would be at the town's only church and they'd already picked out rings at the local jewelry that were being over-sized because the couple had short but very thick fingers.

"Ruff, would you be my best man at the wedding?"

"An honor, sir!"

"Reba will be my maid of honor and I would like you, Dixie, to be my bridesmaid."

"I would be thrilled!"

A short time and two more bottles of wine later, Dolly burped and cried, "Now let's toast to our new territorial capital, Prescott!"

A short time later, Darby asked, "What is going on with Houston?"

Ruff' voice took on a somber tone. "He returned only a short while ago looking like death. He'd gone back to Ash Fork to see Peaches ... I mean Mrs. Patterson ... and it must not have gone well at all."

"Why do you say that? Did you talk with him?"

"No," Dixie answered. "He was dead asleep in the barn and Mando said that he didn't want to be awakened until tomorrow morning. Houston has a gunpowder burn on one hand and blood on a new pair of pants. Mando didn't ask him what had happened, so Ruff and I figured whatever it was could wait until morning. High Man looked hard-used."

Darby scowled. "You brother wouldn't have gotten in a fight with Peaches Patterson and accidentally killed her, would he?"

"My brother would never kill a woman."

"Even in self-defense?"

Both Ruff and Dixie solemnly shook their heads. After a moment, Dixie said, "I could imagine Houston hitting a woman who was trying to kill him just so he could escape her. But Mando said he had powder burns, so we're worried."

"You have plenty of reason to be," Dolly offered. "Was your brother infatuated with the young widow?"

"Maybe," Ruff admitted. "And he sort of had in mind asking her to help us buy a ranch. We found one out near Fort Whipple that we think would work, but its considerably more expensive than we can afford."

Darby and Dolly exchanged glances before the dime novelist grew impatient and asked, "Are you planning to tell us about it?"

"It's a thousand acres of bottomland fronted by Granite Creek. Good grass in the spring right into fall. Several years ago, it was attacked and burned out by Indians ..." Dixie looked at the pretty half-breed girl. "I don't know if was attacked by your people or others."

"What is the name of the ranch?" Reba asked softly.

"River Ranch."

Reba quickly left the table.

"I guess it must have been at least some of her people," Dixie said softly. "A family and some hired hands were massacred. The livestock were all butchered or stolen."

"Perhaps," Darby said, "you should look elsewhere for property. This ranch definitely has a bad aura."

"True enough, but it's about the land," Ruff explained. "Not its ruined house or barns. Those can all be replaced. And as for the bloody history, without it, this place would have sold long ago. We met the bank manager. They hold the title and it is for sale for three thousand dollars."

After a moment, Darby asked, "How much do you actually need to rebuild and fix up the stables, barns and pastures?"

"A lot. We also need enough money for a professional racetrack," Dixie told the Derby Man. "We plan to invite people to race their horses and, of course, we will take a fee."

"Race against your Thoroughbreds?" Dolly asked. "Who would be foolish enough to do that?"

"You can make the betting odds even," Ruff explained. "For example, depending on the length of the race, you can allow a slower horse a certain advantage. Say a hundred yards over a mile race."

"Or more against our Thoroughbreds," Dixie quickly added. "The point is that you make the lead distance for the slower horse long enough to ensure that it has a chance to win."

"And why would you do that?"

"Again, so the betting odds would be near even," Ruff explained. "But we'd know the track better than anyone and that would give us a slight advantage. If our horses won every race, no one would race, much less bet. And in that case, no money could be made."

"I'm beginning to understand," Dolly said. "It's all a little chancy if you are up against a slower horse but give it too much of a head start."

"Yes, but Dixie can ride and race High Fire for quite a few more years. And in three years we'll have new Thoroughbred stallion to race. People with racing in their blood will want our bloodlines to build their own stables in places like California, Colorado and New Mexico."

"You've obviously put a lot of thought to this," Darby said, eyeing the apple pie and then slicing himself a thick wedge.

"We learned it from our father back in Tennessee," Ruff confessed. "We learned that a smart racehorse stable doesn't always want its horse to win."

"Surely you wouldn't throw a race … would you?" Dolly asked with alarm.

"Never," Dixie assured her. "If you hold back a champion and keep it from winning then you may ruin its racing spirit forever. It would be a sacrilege, a travesty and completely dishonest."

"So once again," Darby asked, "how much money is required for the ranch and to rebuild everything, including putting in a fine racetrack?"

Ruff and Dixie exchanged quick glances. Ruff took a deep breath and said, "To buy the land, rebuild the house, erect a large new barn, corrals and the racetrack would probably take at least ten thousand dollars. But it wouldn't have to all be done at once."

Dixie quickly added, "We have about a thousand dollars and we were hoping that Peaches Patterson would find the idea of partly owning a stable appealing enough to …"

"Forget that dingy woman," Darby said shortly. "She would be a terrible partner. Dolly and I will make far better ones."

Dixie clapped her hands with delight. "That's wonderful news! We had wondered if you just might want to invest."

Darby thought a moment and said, "For half ownership in everything *except* the horses we're willing to add ten thousand dollars to your one thousand, so we can build *two* houses!"

"*Two* houses?" Ruff asked in surprise.

"Yes," Dolly said. "Because Darby and I want a lovely place to live for ourselves … and for Mando and Reba. So, we're going to need a good-sized house … at least four bedrooms."

"Then I'm afraid ten … we might need a little more money," Ruff mused.

"That's fine," Dolly told him. "I have amassed enough savings to add to the pot and I insist on doing that so that I can feel I am doing my part."

Darby smiled. "And what else would I spend my money on? I've made a small fortune and I've lived within my means for many years. It's time I settled down with the woman I love. And when we get itchy feet and want to travel to the big cities, the pair of you can care for and look after our house and property."

"How generous and exciting," Dixie said.

"Yes," Darby agreed. "And we hope you would allow us to invest in a few of your most promising young animals to make it more interesting when we place wagers at our races."

"Of course!" Dixie exclaimed. "But you know we would have to ask Houston for his approval."

"Ask him, although it sounds to me like he is not going to be in any position to refuse our offer," Darby said. "And I am now really curious as to what kind of trouble your brother got himself into while he was in Ash Fork. But that most certainly can wait until morning."

"Until Houston has a breakfast and a few cups of coffee," Dixie added, "my brother is not agreeable."

"Understood," Darby said. "So, tomorrow Dolly and I will start making plans for our marriage and getting our finances together for the Prescott National Bank."

"And what about Reba?" Dixie asked, glancing toward the door where she'd disappeared. "Given the history of this ranch we're going to buy, do you think she and Mando could even live with us?"

"Good question. One of so many," Darby said. "And if we can pull this all together, what is the name of the ranch to be?"

"River Ranch," Ruff said quickly.

"Ghost Ranch," Dixie countered.

There was a long moment of silence and then Dolly said, "Given the sad history and feelings of Reba and Mando ... it will have to be an entirely different name. Ghost Ranch would be a constant and painful reminder to our young friends of the bloodshed, and River Ranch would always be a cross for them to bear."

Ruff shrugged. "That makes sense. I can't think of anything else to call it."

"*I'll* name our ranch," Darby said with a smile. "I'm the writer, remember?"

"And the one with the most money," Dolly added.

The two young Ballou people nodded in agreement because the reasoning made perfectly good sense and now, they wouldn't have to argue about the horse ranch's name anymore.

CHAPTER 17

Darby and Dolly were so excited about their upcoming marriage and ranch plans that they couldn't sleep so they went outside and rocked on the front porch until well after midnight. They were just about to go to bed when four riders appeared out of the darkness, slowly coming up Union Street in the faint moonlight.

Dolly stopped rocking. "Good heavens, what ..."

"Shhh!" Darby hissed, slipping back into the house dressed only in his bathrobe and slippers. Moments later, he appeared with his new shotgun and he cocked its hammers.

"Darby, darling! Are you going to shoot them *all?"*

"Probably not," Darby said. "Slip inside the house and make sure that Reba isn't wandering around. Both of you stay low."

"But ..."

"Just do it," Darby ordered in a hushed voice as he moved in behind a tall, climbing rose bush and waited to see what would happen next.

The riders stopped and reined their mounts toward the house. Darby held his breath and heard them cock their pistols.

Enough! he thought, whipping the shotgun up and unleashing a tremendous double barrel blast aimed just over the riders.

His action sparked an immediate reaction. All of the horses were so spooked they whirled and two of them went off bucking down the street until their riders were tossed. The other pair managed to stay astride their mounts and spurred them as if the Devil himself was nipping at their heels.

Darby leaned the shotgun against the house and Dolly rushed back out to hug his neck. "What was that about!"

"I think they were meaning to shoot out all of your front windows this time," Darby said grimly as he noticed lights going on in some of the nearby houses and people rushing outside to see what had caused the commotion. The two men who'd been bucked off staggered down the street chasing their horses and one was limping so badly Darby figured he'd busted or badly bruised a knee or a leg.

Reba appeared. "They were here because of me. They want to know where my father's gold mine is, and we won't tell them. Maybe I should go. I am putting you both in danger."

"Please stay," Dolly said earnestly. "And we won't be living here much longer."

Darby said, "I'm sure you know we are buying that place that used to be called the River Ranch and we're going to turn it into a new horse ranch with its very own racetrack. We want you and Mando come and live there with us."

Reba touched Dolly's shoulder, "Are you are going to live on the ranch, too?"

"Yes, and we want you and your brother to be a part of our family."

It was hard to see much in the darkness, but they both heard Reba's little cry of relief and happiness.

"Oh yes! Me and my brother, Mando, will come with you!"

"Then that's settled," Darby announced. "And I was wondering what you women thought about renaming the place *Far West Thoroughbred Ranch.*"

Dolly shook her head. "How about Prescott *Thoroughbred Ranch?*"

"Reba, do you have any names you want to toss in the pot?"

"I like *Happy Horse Ranch.*"

"Not bad. So now we have four names besides the original River Ranch. We have *Ghost Ranch, Far West Thoroughbred Ranch, Prescott Thoroughbred Ranch* and *Happy Horse Ranch.*"

"We can take a vote after we buy the place," Dolly said.

"Makes a lot of sense."

Dolly moved back into her kitchen. "Darby, did you recognize any of those four riders?"

"No. Too dark. If we could find them tonight, they'd be the ones with poop in their pants or a broken leg. I think that shotgun blast near scared them out of their wits."

"They might come back." Dolly was cutting up

the rest of the uneaten apple pie. "And if they do ..."

"Next time I won't aim for the sky" Darby said grimly. "And maybe I should talk to the marshal again."

"I'm not sure that's such a good idea," Dolly said, "after all, he might even have been one of them."

"That's true," Darby said, reloading. "We've got to be vigilant until we can move out to the new place and start building. Reba, what do your people use for shelter?"

"Wikiups. They're brush covered and ..."

"That won't work," Darby interrupted. "We'll figure out something better in a hurry. As soon as it gets a little warmer, we'll move."

"But first we have to buy the ranch," Dolly reminded them both.

"Yes, as the yet nameless ranch on Granite Creek."

"That's it!" Dolly cried. "If the Ballou family agrees, let's call it *Granite Creek Ranch.*"

"That suits me just fine." The Derby Man glanced over at Reba. "Okay with you?"

"Sure."

"Good." Darby yawned. The bottles of wine were having their effect.

Late the next morning, Houston showed up at Dolly's door and was invited inside. The gunpowder burn on his hand was inflamed and he was out of sorts. "I didn't get very far with Peaches. Turns out that Patterson had a son and he's claiming the inheritance. To save all the fuss and expense of lawyers, Peaches and he are getting married."

"I suppose Ruff and Dixie told you that we're getting married as well," Dolly said. "And you're certainly invited to attend what will be a small, private and simple ceremony."

"With cake and champagne," Darby added. "Not French, but a California vintage and quite acceptable."

"Thanks." Houston reached into his pocket and pulled out the Wanted Poster. "It seems that a few members of the Confederacy are still after us and in search of revenge."

"Five hundred dollars each is an impressive bounty," Darby said. "But that's a very poor sketch of you and Ruff."

Houston chuckled. "Not in the least bit flattering, I'd say. We're both far handsomer."

"Yes," Dolly agreed, "you most certainly are. And perhaps there will be no more bounty hunters."

"Not something we dare to count on, Miss Beavers. And I have been thinking about going back to Tennessee. Maybe finding out who's behind the reward and putting a stop to it. And perhaps seeing if I can get some money for restitution in the matter of our land and properties now being held by carpetbaggers."

Darby shook his head. "It's unlikely that you'd have any success in the matter of financial restitution."

"You never know until you try," Houston replied. He got up and headed outside. "I'm going to ride out and look at the River Ranch."

"Granite Creek Ranch," Dolly corrected. "And we're going to be partners."

"Yeah." Houston managed a smile. "That's what I heard. I'm real happy we're going to be partners in all property except ownership of the Ballou Thoroughbreds."

"Nice hat and boots," Darby told the man.

"Not nice enough to win Peaches but they sure impressed a pretty little gal named Lula May."

Houston climbed on High Fire and headed on down the street.

"He sure a fine figure on a horse," Dolly said with a cluck of her tongue.

"But not as fine as I do."

"I was just going to say that," Dolly offered with a coy smile. "When do you want to go to the bank and see about getting the paperwork started?"

"The sooner the better."

Dolly nodded and went inside to grab her purse.

The Prescott National Bank wasn't impressive, and neither was its manager, Robert Tillman. Darby and Dolly were offered seats at his desk and stated that they were ready to buy the River Ranch.

Tillman made quite a show of regret. "Well, I'm real sorry to tell you that we've sold it already."

"Is that right," Darby said, thick black mustache bristling. "When and to whom?"

"Uh, yesterday."

"Who bought it?"

The banker squirmed. "No offense, Mr. Buckingham, but I don't think that's any of your business."

"Oh, but it is," Darby countered with a definite

edge to his voice. "I need to see the paperwork on the sale, or I'll be forced to take legal action."

Tillman's smile turned sour. "Oh, you would now, would you?"

"Since arriving here I've met some of the town's leading citizens as well as a few of the territorial officials. I'm sure you know Mr. Pennington, our new territorial judge. Just so happens that he just loves my dime novels and is quite a fan. I expect he wouldn't hesitate to come over here right now and take a look at the paperwork."

Tillman shifted uneasily in his fancy desk chair. "Well, we actually haven't signed anything quite yet."

"Then Miss Beavers and I will start that process right now," Darby said, lighting up one of his fine cigars before offering another to the banker who snatched it from his grasp when he saw it was imported from Cuba.

"Thank you. I'll get my assistant over here and we can start the paperwork. Will the ranch property be in both your names?"

"It will be in our names as well as the three members of the Ballou family," Dolly said. "They'll be in to sign papers later."

The banker nodded and bit the end off the expensive cigar. "Three thousand dollars. One thousand acres with good water. Nice buy on the River Ranch. Very good buy."

"We think so too," Dolly said, "and we're renaming it the *Granite Creek Ranch.*"

"Of course! It's just a name, right?"

Darby blew a cloud of smoke in the banker's

face then leaned back in his chair, smiling with satisfaction.

Once the signing was finished and a deposit paid, Darby and Dolly left the Prescott National Bank and headed for the jewelry store to look at their rings, and then visit the church and set up a small ceremony.

They were just outside when Marshal Richard Judd met them. "Well," he said forcing a cold grin, "aren't you the pair of lovebirds."

"Are you limping?" Darby asked.

"No. Why do you ask?"

"Four men came by Miss Beaver's house last night with evil intentions. I showed them what a shotgun could do, and their horses did a wild dance in the street. Two were thrown, one was badly injured and went limping up Union Street."

Judd snorted. "And you think I was one of them?"

"Wouldn't surprise me."

"You have a helluva lot of nerve speaking to me that way."

"You haven't seen anything yet if you mess with our family," Dolly warned.

"What *family?*"

"Miss Beavers and I are getting married in a few days. We won't be inviting you to the wedding, but even so, aren't you going to at least congratulate us?"

The marshal's eyes tightened at the corners and his lips formed a hard, pale line a moment before he stomped away.

"Damn," Darby muttered, "I was sure hoping he'd be limping this morning."

"One thing I'm quite curious about," Dolly said. "Is the new territorial judge, this man Pennington, really a huge fan of your dime novels?"

Darby inhaled cigar smoke and blew it out into the cool, clean air. "Well, my dear, if he isn't, he sure ought to be."

A moment later, they were both laughing.

CHAPTER 18

The day before the wedding, Darby was working on the last chapter of his new dime novel when there was a knock on the cottage door. Dolly and Reba had gone shopping in town and Darby didn't like to be interrupted when he was writing, but the knocking was persistent.

"Damn," Darby muttered as he laid his pen down and went to answer the door.

"Mr. Darby Buckingham!" Homer Gentry exclaimed. "I am sorry to interrupt but I just had to come over as soon as my wife and I got into Prescott to say hello."

Darby liked the former Ash Fork editor and invited him into Dolly's parlor. "You've arrived in Prescott sooner than planned."

"That's right. My term as mayor of Ash Fork still has a week left, but the city council let me go early. They have a good man to replace me, so my wife and I saw no reason to delay coming to Prescott. This town is buzzing with activity and it's where we want to plant our roots."

"What about work? Did you bring your printing press?"

"I did not. I sold it and the building to a new publisher, a much younger man. The press would have been difficult to move and when my editor friend at the *Daily Miner* said he really wanted me to go to work as his partner I thought that was the best solution."

"Welcome to Arizona's territorial capital. Is your wife outside?"

"No, she's already gadding about the plaza meeting new friends and asking other women where this or that can be found at the most reasonable price."

"Have you found a place to live?"

"We'll stay at the hotel until we find something we want to buy. We don't need a big house. Maybe something like this place."

"It's my fiancé's cottage," Darby said.

"It's very nice … other than the purple color. Sure stands out from anything else in this town."

Darby managed to suppress a smile. "It certainly does."

"Will you be living here permanently?"

"No, Miss Beavers and I will be getting married this Saturday and as soon as a ranch sale closes, we'll be moving just north of town."

"My oh my!" Gentry exclaimed. "Getting married, moving and … he peered around Darby's broad shoulders to a table strewn with manuscript paper. "Pray tell, Mr. Buckingham, is that your latest dime novel?"

"It is. Almost completed."

Gentry beamed. "And I probably interrupted your writing. I'm so sorry and I won't take up any more of your valuable time."

"Homer, I'm pleased that you made the move to Prescott and once we get settled, I'll be more than happy to give you another interview focusing on my new novel, *Santa Fe Showdown.* It won't be published for a month or two, but as soon as it is made available, I'm assuming your friend at the *Daily Miner* would be happy to give me a little local promotion."

"Of course!"

"Also, my fiancé and I would like you and your wife to attend our wedding this Saturday. One o'clock in the afternoon at the Episcopalian Church. It's going to be a very small and intimate affair and there will be refreshments afterward."

"We'd love to attend, and my wife will be thrilled. We haven't had the pleasure of attending a wedding in years. Just funerals in Ash Fork and they were pretty sad affairs. Speaking of which, there is an important funeral this Saturday."

Darby's eyebrows raised in question. "A close friend of yours?"

"No, I hardly knew the young man. I'm sure that you well remember Mister and Missus Patterson."

"Of course," Darby said. "Either I or Dixie shot him dead in the street. Patterson was a very violent man. We killed him in self-defense."

"Everyone understood that," the editor assured him. "The shootout was witnessed by a lot of people and no one held you or the Ballou girl responsible. You were simply forced to shoot first or be killed."

"Then ..."

"As you probably also remember, everyone in Ash Fork expected his widow, Mrs. Peaches Patterson, to inherit the town's only mercantile store along with some other properties. Well, things have turned out quite differently than everyone expected."

"Yes, Houston told me a little about a sudden and unexpected development."

"Then you probably know that Patterson hadn't left a will, so we all thought that Peaches was certain to become a very wealthy young woman. Then, within days of the funeral, a dapper young fellow named Peter Patterson arrived who had proof that he was sole and legal heir to the entire estate."

"I imagine it was quite a shock."

"That is an understatement, Mr. Buckingham. And at first, young Peter Patterson seemed nice, and when he and Peaches got married everyone in Ash Fork thought they would make a fine couple and do a lot of good for our town. But apparently young Mr. Patterson had inherited from his father a very dark side and he soon began drinking and beating his bride."

"That's a real pity."

"Yes, it is. Peaches would hide in shame because her lovely face was often badly bruised. Some people who lived near her and her new husband said they could hear the newlyweds fighting and shouting every night. And then one evening the domestic fight escalated into gunfire. Peaches shot and killed

Peter. Shot him twice in the face and twice more in his ... well, his nether region."

Darby was not a man easily shaken but now he did need to take a chair. "I remember her so very well. I liked Peaches and felt sorry for the way she was treated by her first—and much older—husband."

"Well apparently the apple did not fall far from the tree, because his son was every bit as violent as the old man. But there were no witnesses and the fact that Peaches obviously shot him twice in his previously handsome face and then in his crotch made the circuit judge think it had been a case of rage and *murder.*"

"But if Mrs. Patterson shot her new husband to save her life ... or to prevent further beatings ... then I don't see why she be charged with murder rather than self-defense."

Homer Gentry nodded. "It seems that Peter Patterson had met the circuit judge and secretly had made a deal that he would relieve Peaches of her property. I think he was planning to divorce her and marry a wanton woman named Lula May Garfield."

"What a sinister, complex web of deceit!" Darby exclaimed.

"Yes, and that's why my wife and I wanted to leave Ash Fork as quickly as possible. There will be a murder trial and who knows what will happen? There being no witnesses but only the desecrated face of the deceased, I'm afraid that the outcome of the trial will not be in Mrs. Patterson's favor."

Darby Buckingham was relieved that he and the Ballou people had left Ash Fork before the shooting death had occurred. However, after the trial and verdict, it might be something he could use in his next novel.

"Well," the former editor and mayor of Ash Fork said, "I need to leave you to your writing and go find my wife before she buys up half the downtown."

"Thank you for coming by and filling me in on all that business. Very interesting and disturbing."

"How very true and completely unexpected by everyone." Gentry waved his hand as if to dismiss the dark thoughts and said, "But now my wife and I will get to enjoy the pleasure of your wedding. We can hardly wait to meet your new wife, sir."

"She's a real character," Darby warned. "Dolly says whatever is on her mind and she is not the least bit bashful."

"I'll bet she suits you well." The editor looked around for a moment. "Earlier you said that you and your soon to be wife were moving a short distance north. What will happen to this cottage?"

"I expect that Dolly will put it up for sale."

"If that is the case, please consider giving me and my wife the first chance to make a fair offer. We'd repaint the place right off, of course."

Darby chuckled. "And just between the two of us, I'd do the same."

After the editor left, Darby sat back down at the table to resume writing, but his mind was just not on the novel. He was deeply troubled by the killing in Ash Fork and the impending possibility that Peaches might actually be convicted of murder.

Their wedding was quick and simple. Dolly had found a lovely pink dress with a white veil and shiny brown shoes. Darby had been unable to find a decent tuxedo anywhere close to his dimensions, so he had his best black suit cleaned and pressed. They made an impressive pair, and afterward there had been many hearty toasts to the health and happiness of the new couple. Besides the Ballou people, Reba, Mando, Homer Gentry and his wife and the jolly minister who drank more champagne than anyone, there were only a few of Dolly's new friends.

Dolly fairly glowed after the wedding. "I have loved you so long and now I am dancing on air!"

"My love, we've lived through many adventures—some good and some not—in search of my stories. I should have married you years ago."

"Yes," she agreed, "but I forgive you. Do you regret that we are probably not going to be able to have children because ... well, because I am past that time?"

"Not at all," he said, meaning it. "I most enjoy children when they belong to someone else. Did you actually *want* children?"

"I suppose I would have liked a little Darby or two ... but I'm fine with just you and me being together until 'death do us part.'"

"In that case," the dime novelist said, "let's just hope that we have a long, healthy life together."

Suddenly the church door slammed open with a bang. "So, the lovebirds tied the knot!" Marshal Judd shouted, stumbling into the church hall. "I had to see it with my own eyes."

"The man is dead drunk," Dolly whispered as the room fell silent. "And he's going to get nasty."

"No," Darby assured her, "he is going to get *unconscious.*"

Darby crossed the hall in four quick steps and just as the marshal was about to speak again the dime novelist smashed him with a powerful uppercut to the jaw that dropped him like a stone.

"Let's get him out of here," Darby growled to no one in particular.

Houston grabbed a leg, so did Ruff and with Darby grasping the unconscious man's arms, they dragged the marshal out of the church and into the middle of the street where they dropped and left him for everyone in town to see.

"You might just have killed him with one punch," Houston said not bothering to hide his admiration. "That was a wicked blow."

"He deserved it." Darby patted the man's shoulder. "I just heard from Homer Gentry that Peaches is in jail facing a murder charge for shooting her young husband to death. I know that you had feelings for her and I'm sorry how it all turned out."

Houston paled slightly then turned on his heel and swiftly headed for the stable barn.

"Where's he going!" Ruff asked, looking after his brother.

"I expect he's going back to Ash Fork to see if he can help Peaches Patterson."

"Excuse me for making a quick exit," Ruff said. "But I know my brother and he's headed for trouble… maybe even death."

"You really think you can stop him?" Darby asked.

"No. But I can give him a little advice that might save him a world of grief."

Ruff hurried after his brother. Dixie and several others came out from the church to stare at the unconscious lawman.

"Darling," Dolly whispered, coming up to take his arm, "we did pay for a fiddler and there is a lot of champagne left to drink. Won't you please come back inside to our reception? This will only happen once."

Darby took a deep breath and escorted his bride back into the church hall wondering what Ruff could possibly say to help his big brother.

"You're not taking High Man back to Ash Fork again," Ruff said from the barn's doorway. "He's still worn down from your last run over there."

Houston turned and faced his brother. "So now you're trying to tell me what Ballou horse I can or can't ride?"

"In this case, I am. You know that that our old champion deserves his rest and that I won't allow you to risk laming High Fire."

"And the mares are all in foal," Houston spat. "So where does that leave me ... hiking all the way over to Ash Fork?"

"Buy yourself an ordinary saddle horse. There are a few right outside in the corral. Pick one and ride into whatever hornet's nest you intend to stir up in Ash Fork."

Houston stood there teetering on a decision.

Finally, his body relaxed, and he said, "Alright. I'll buy good traveling horse."

"Thank you." In truth, Ruff did not know what he would have done to stop his brother and so he was greatly relieved.

"I'll be back one day."

"Don't get shot or hanged, Brother. Peaches didn't choose you when she had the chance ... instead she chose money. Just keep reminding yourself of that fact."

"Tell Dixie I may not come back for a long time. I have to go to Tennessee and settle things. I don't want us to always be looking over our shoulders for a bunch of ex-Confederate bounty hunters."

"We've done fine so far."

"We're not running anymore. We're taking a stand right here in Prescott. We'll be easy to find when word spreads about our horse ranch and racetrack. I need to settle things permanently."

Ruff could see that there was nothing he could say or do to change Houston's mind. Besides, what his older brother said was true.

"Good luck."

"Same to you," Houston replied. "I don't know how long I'll be gone but when I do return, I'll expect our ranch house to be rebuilt and the barns, corrals and everything else to be in first rate shape. And I'll also expect you and Dixie to have gotten off with a good start on this new crop of foals."

"I guarantee they will be."

Houston winked. "So, you see, my decision is all about avoiding hard, physical work."

"I figured that was a big part of it."

They hugged then and Ruff went back to the wedding reception wondering if he would ever see his last—his *only*—brother again.

When Houston rode a fast walking buckskin gelding into Ash Fork, he went straight to the sheriff's office and met the town's new lawman, Sheriff Jack Gunter. Gunter was a hard-looking man with a hook nose, big ears and some nasty scars on his long face. The first thought Houston had was that the town's new lawman looked like the east end of a westbound jackass. And there was a powerful odor of liquor on his breath.

"I remember you," Gunter said. "What are you doing back here?"

"I come to see Missus Patterson."

"Well, there she is," Sheriff Gunter drawled, jacking his thumb over his shoulder toward a cramped jail cell. "She ain't as pretty as she used to be and not nearly so high and mighty."

"I need to talk to her in private."

"Too bad. I'm not going anywhere."

"How about you go buy yourself a bottle of whiskey on me?" Houston said, pulling out some money. "Find a quiet hiding place to drink."

Gunter's eyes narrowed. "You want to poke Peaches right here in the jail?"

"I sure do."

The sheriff grinned showing bad teeth. "I reckon you're going to have yourself a high old time with that one."

Houston felt the rage build up into his throat and then he realized what he needed to do next. Not just talk to Peaches and try to figure out how to save her, but to actually spring her from this crap hole and take her to faraway places.

"Okay," he said, peeling off ten dollars. That ought to buy at least two bottles. Just don't come back until tomorrow morning."

Sheriff Gunter laughed, leering back at the cell. "You got a big appetite for that widow, huh?"

"Sheriff, are you going take my money and go … or not?"

"Key to the cell is on the wall over yonder." Gunter's hand snaked out and he took the money. He jammed on his old hat and headed out the door looking back at Houston. "I hope you get every penny of your damned money's worth!"

"Peaches," Houston said, hurrying back to the dim, dirty cell. "What the hell kind of a fix have you gotten yourself into now?"

"I shot Peter dead and if you try to rape me in this cell, I will figure a way to kill you."

"I'm not here for that."

"Oh, yeah, then what, my money?" She laughed bitterly. "It's all tied up by the circuit judge. I haven't got a cent."

"I have over a hundred dollars," Houston told her, turning the lock and stepping back as the protesting cell door swung open. "Do you want to leave Ash Fork forever?"

Peaches was so taken by surprise at the question that she stood still for a long moment. "You want to take *me* away?"

"Sure! I've always had a hunger and admiration for you. So, do you want to put the dust of Ash Fork far behind us?"

"If I do, I'll lose almost everything. And if I go with you then you'll just use me ... probably beat me like my last two husbands and then I'll be left to fend for myself in some miserable little town. That doesn't sound so good."

"I've never beaten a woman in my life and I never will," Houston answered. "I'm not saying I'll marry you. I'll make you no grand promises except to say that I'll take care of you for as long as I can. And if I leave you, it'll be in a good place with some money, not dead broke in a bad one."

"Why?"

Houston thought about that for a moment. "I know what you did, and I admire a woman who has the sand to stand up for herself. And as you are well aware, you're one of the most beautiful women in Arizona."

Her fingers touched her swollen, bruised face. "Not anymore."

"But you will be again when the swelling and discoloration in your face goes away. Peaches, I'm offering you my word to treat you right and I don't care if you own nothing but the clothes you are wearing."

"Where are you fixin' to go? Back to Prescott?"

"No, I'm bound for Tennessee."

A slow and obviously painful smile came over her battered face. "My oh my! I have never been to the South."

"It's beautiful, and my family has a horse ranch. Prettiest piece of property you would ever lay eyes upon. Prettier than anything for a thousand miles in any direction from Ash Fork."

"Well, if you promise to take me all the way to Tennessee, I'd like to ride along. We'd see new country and we'd make a fine pair working all the saloons."

"Then let's stop talking and start moving."

He reached out and took her upper arm, but she instinctively jerked back like a mare that has been abused hard and often.

"Easy," Houston said softly, "you have my word that your hurtin' days are behind you now."

Peaches must have believed him because she let him lead her out of the jail cell.

"Can you ride?" he asked.

"Like a tick on a running dog."

"Then all I have to do now is steal you a good horse. There are a couple hitched up outside."

"I've got my own good horse in a corral behind my house. I want my own saddle, too."

"It's a little more dangerous to go there."

"Let's take the risk. I've got a hell of a lot of cash hidden in my attic."

Houston's eyebrows raised. "I thought you said that if you left here with me on the run, you'd lose everything and have nothing."

"I lied to see if you were only interested in my money. Fact is, when I knew that I was going to have to kill Peter to save my life, I started secretly cashing in whatever I could lay my hands upon. I did it secretly through a woman friend. I accumulated a bundle of cash knowing I'd have to kill Peter and go on the run."

"So, you're *still* a wealthy woman?"

She managed a painful, lopsided smile. "Not nearly as wealthy as I'd have been if Peter hadn't suddenly appeared, but wealthy enough."

"Damn! That's real good!"

They started for the door, but the woman stopped. "Houston, there's a fine rifle and couple of pistols in the gun case. I'll get me some of the sheriff's ammunition, too ... just in case a posse might catch up with us and we have to kill them."

"I like the way you think ahead, Peaches."

"You ain't seen the half of what you'll like about me," she promised him as she went over to pick out weapons.

Less than an hour later, as a full, luminous moon slipped up over Big Black Mesa, Houston and Peaches rode west at a quick trot. Houston knew it was the best way to cover a lot of ground over a long spell without exhausting your mount.

"Dammit, Houston, this mare's hard trot is shakin' my *tits* off!" Peaches finally cried in protest.

"Well, that'd be a helluva shame."

Houston laughed at the moon, touched spurs and put his buckskin into an easy, ground-eating lope, and Peaches galloped up right beside him.

CHAPTER 19

By the time Spring arrived in Prescott, construction and repair of the Granite Creek Ranch was well underway. Darby and Dolly's home on their five hundred acres sat on a low rise of land and was constructed of timber locally logged, planed and dried by the Pioneer Sawmill. The house itself was a single level, with five bedrooms and a spacious office for Darby to use writing his dime novels. Their house had a wide veranda on three sides with their best view to the west toward the towering Granite Mountains. They also had a small building constructed to contain Dolly's gardening supplies and soil amendments, in addition to a chicken house and goat barn.

The former burned-out main ranch house that was now the new home of the Ballou family and it boasted two stories and four bedrooms. The original main ranch house had been completely rebuilt around the old, massive stone fireplace. The flooring had been repaired and was now entirely of the beautiful flagstone found up around Ash Fork. The parlor was small, but the kitchen and dining rooms were enormous. Neither Dixie or Ruff were particularly interested in their new house and were surprised that the half-breed girl, Reba, had very good ideas about how the interior of the big house should be laid out.

"If you and Mando lived in a wikiup as children," Dixie asked, "how do you know about such things as furnishing for a house?"

"I said that my people, the Yavapai, lived in wikiups, but we never did. My father built a mining shack up on Granite Mountain and we sometimes we stayed in town to help people with their domestic chores in order to earn extra money. There were a few ladies that I cleaned for and they liked nothing better than to tell me about how they picked their furnishings. Some of their most prized possessions came from the East, some from San Francisco. I saw a clock that was from some place called Germany and it was beautiful. The first time the bird came flying out to cuckoo, I nearly fainted dead away. Mainly though, I just worked, listened closely to them and learned."

Dixie soon discovered that Reba was also a very good shot. She and her brother had been expected by their often-drunken father to hunt and provide meat. But what was almost as surprising to Dixie about the half-breed girl was that Reba loved horses and would beg her to go riding and be allowed to watch the Thoroughbred mares deliver their newborns with the help of her brother, Mando.

"The sooner we get the barn and all the stalls inside finished, the better all this will go," Dixie fretted. "We've got three foals now and two more on the way. I worry about bears and cougars coming down from the mountains at night and slaughtering them."

"We should get some fierce guard dogs," Reba said. "I know someone who raises them."

"Where?"

Reba pointed up into the wilderness. "He is an old man, but his dogs are prized by my people. They are big, strong and brave. He breeds and raises them for people who have sheep."

"Can we ride to this place and back in a day?" Dixie asked.

"If we start early. But I cannot promise he will have any puppies or young dogs for sale."

"If he doesn't, we can at least let him know we want a couple. I know that Dolly wants a big dog as well although I sense that Darby is not all that keen on the idea."

Reba giggled. "Dolly will run that house and get what she wants even though Mr. Buckingham *thinks* he rules the roost."

"Is that how you read it?"

Reba grinned and nodded her head.

"We'll go see this old Indian dog-raiser tomorrow," Dixie told her new friend. "Let's walk over to see Dolly and tell her about it and make sure she hasn't changed her mind. If she hasn't, we'll be wanting three dogs."

In the morning, they saddled a pair of riding horses that had been purchased from nearby Fort Whipple. They were good mounts but older, retired cavalry animals, well-broke, slow and boring to ride. Mostly Ruff had bought them because being older, they were cheap, steady and well trained. Just in the few months that the Ballou family had owned them they had put on at least 150 pounds each and were now a little on the tubby side, making them even slower.

"Say hello to *Ida-heh,"* Mando said when his sister had told them about she and Dixie going up to the mountains.

"I will."

It was only a little after daybreak when they left the Granite Creek Ranch and headed west, gradually climbing up through the pinion and juniper dotted foothills. They didn't see any antelope or deer and when Dixie commented on that fact, Reba explained, "When I was a little girl there were many deer and antelope. Black bear and big elk, too. But when gold and silver was discovered and all the miners started coming into our country, they shot out the wild animals to eat. Now, I think you have to go far up in the mountains."

Around mid-morning they came upon an old cabin and some broken down corrals. The roof was burned out and so was a shed. Reba grew sad and silent.

"I take it you know this place," Dixie said.

"It was our place. My mother and father are buried over there." Reba pointed to a small, level area already being overtaken by sage and chaparral so that the pair of simple wooden crosses were almost invisible.

"Would you like to spend a little time with them?"

"No. They are gone now except for their spirits. I feel a coldness when my father's spirit is close but grow warm again when my mother's spirit is near."

"I feel the same way about my mother's Cherokee spirit. We'd better ride on now."

Reba urged her horse on up the mountain into a thick pine forest. She rode with her head down no doubt lost in a cloud of sad childhood memories.

At a small outcropping of rocks, Reba tied her horse to a scrubby pinion pine and climbed up the rocks to look around. Dixie dismounted to follow her.

"Are we lost?" Dixie asked.

"I know this country very well. But I have the feeling we are being *followed."*

"By who?"

"The men who want to steal all the gold from our family's mine."

They climbed on top of boulder and looked down into Williamson Valley. Then suddenly, Reba exclaimed, "There! Four riders!"

Dixie was shocked because the four men following their trail were within a mile.

"Dammit, we should have brought rifles!" She scrambled off the boulder and hurried to her horse. "I have an old pistol in my saddlebag, but it only has six bullets."

"And I don't have any kind of a weapon," Reba

lamented. "Let's mount up and go!"

"Where?"

"To the cave where we mined gold. It is well hidden."

"But we can't hide these old Army horses!"

"And we can't outrun them, Dixie. So, what is left?"

"We leave the horses here, take the pistol and hike to your gold mine and hide in it. If they find the mine's entrance and come in after us and I'll shoot as many as I can. Four men, six bullets. It might work."

"I have a knife," Reba said. "Let's run! The mine is only a little way up this mountain. The old Indian with the dogs is not far away either."

"Maybe we should try to reach him and . . ."

"No," Reba said flatly. "They would shoot *Ida-heh* and all of his dogs. We would only bring them death."

Dixie was in good physical shape, but they were soon scrambling up a rocky mountainside and the elevation was probably around seven thousand feet. They were both out of breath. Once, they looked back and saw the riders pushing their horses past Reba's old shack and coming up the trail fast.

"There," Reba said, gasping for air and pointing. "Behind those rocks!"

Dixie couldn't see the mouth of the cave, but she was too tired even to slow down knowing that their pursuers were closing.

Reba scrambled over the rocks and disappeared. Dixie followed and a moment later a rifle shot boomed.

"Hurry!" Reba shouted.

Dixie plunged through a hole in the side of the mountain that was no more than four feet high. It was pitch black inside, but Reba found a kerosene lantern and quickly got it lit.

"How far back does your tunnel go?"

"Only about thirty feet. It dog-legs just ahead."

"Then we're trapped!"

"We'd already be dead out there now that they've found this gold mine!"

Dixie knew this was true. She followed Reba closely and then the angle of the mine bent sharply to the right. "We just followed a thin ribbon of gold," Reba explained, rushing on until they came to a small cavern where boxes were stacked amidst empty tin cans and whiskey bottles.

Dixie un-holstered her gun. "They'll come in after us."

Reba hurried to one of the boxes and tore it open to reveal several sticks of dynamite. "We use this only as a last resort."

"I don't want to be buried here!" Dixie exclaimed in protest.

Reba took one stick of the dynamite and held it up. "I'd rather die in a mine cave in than be used then murdered by those men."

"So what … hush!"

They heard men shouting back and forth at the tunnel's entrance while trying to decide what to do next. Minutes later, they heard them step into the mine. One yelled, "Come out or we'll kill you both!"

Dixie raised her pistol and shouted back, "You're going to have to kill us anyway, so come on!"

"Dim the lantern and be ready to light that fuse," Dixie whispered edging back to where the tunnel dog-legged. "I'll shoot them when they enter."

The first man into the tunnel made a fine, easy target silhouetted against the orb of blue sky and Dixie shot him in the chest. The men outside screamed and cursed then started firing into the tunnel. Bullets began ricocheting in all directions, some toward Reba and the little cavern where they were making their last stand. Dixie figured there was a good chance that a ricocheting bullet would strike the box with dynamite and blow them all to smithereens.

"Reba, light the fuse!" she yelled over her shoulder. "We're going to have to throw dynamite at them!"

Reba rushed to her side, lit the fuse and without a split second of hesitation she leaped out into the center of the tunnel and threw the dynamite as hard as she could with a powerful sidearm motion. The dynamite struck the entrance floor, bounced into the sunlight and exploded. The roar and concussion knocked both young women flying.

And that was the last they felt or saw as a small part of the mountainside came sliding down to cover the mine entrance. In seconds, it buried Reba and Dixie and filled the tunnel with choking dust.

CHAPTER 20

Darkness was falling on the Granite Creek Ranch, but the level of anxiety was rising as fast as a shooting star. Darby, Dolly, Ruff and Mando stood in the yard staring up at the dark outline of Granite Mountain wondering why on earth Dixie and Reba had not returned.

"Reba knows that mountain like the back of her hand," Mando told everyone. "She'd know when she had to leave *Ida-heh's* place in order to get back here before sundown."

"Maybe one of those old Army geldings threw a shoe and went lame," Ruff said, arms crossed on his chest and eyes straining into the twilight. "Or maybe one of the horses fell and was injured or killed on the mountainside."

But Mando shook his head. "The trail is rough and steep but not dangerous. My sister would not allow anything bad to happen."

"But accidents *do* happen," Darby countered. "I don't see any choice but to wait until morning and if they're not here by then we ride up the mountain after them."

"I'd like to see that old Indian and his dogs anyway," Dolly added. "I hope the man has some puppies for sale."

Darby rolled his eyes and the others looked at Dolly like she'd said something awful.

Dolly shrugged. "I'm only saying that I think those girls are fine and I'd like to see the big dogs. What's wrong with that?"

No one had an answer and as the night fell, they gave up the watch and went inside to eat and try to sleep.

In the chilly, half-light of morning and filled with foreboding they saddled up the horses. Being the best horseman, Ruff rode the sometimes-fractious High Fire while Mando rode old High Man. Darby rode a mare that didn't want to leave her foal and Dolly a smaller mare that also fought against leaving her sorrel foal behind. But soon they were climbing the mountain with the sun at their backs. Except for the happy sound of birds and the clatter of hooves striking granite rock, there was only stillness and beauty. Whenever Dolly twisted around to gaze back down on the valley and the line of early budding cottonwoods along Granite Creek, she was reminded of how scenic this long shadow country was and how the views ran on forever.

"Dixie and Reba were being followed by four horsemen," Mando said grimly about two hours after leaving the ranch.

"Why?" Darby asked.

"They think that Dixie and my sister are going up to our hidden gold mine."

That made perfectly good sense to the Derby Man. What other reason would riders have for following Dixie and Reba? Were they the same horsemen who had ridden up Union Street and stopped at the purple cottage, drawing their guns with the intention of shooting Dolly's front windows out? Darby thought it likely and he silently cursed himself for not killing them with the shotgun instead of scaring them and their horses almost witless.

It was almost noon when they saw Dixie and Reba's tied horses. And close by they found three untethered saddle horses standing heads down, reins hanging from their bits.

Mando, being the tracker and riding in front, suddenly raised his hand and dismounted. He went over first to Dixie and Reba's old ex-Army horses. "No blood on their saddles."

"What about those three mounts?" Darby asked.

Mando approached the other three horses who seemed spooky and badly frightened. Speaking calmly to the animals he was able to collect their reins and then inspected their saddles.

"Busted reins but no blood."

"How do you read this?" Ruff asked, already having formed his own grim opinion.

Mando thought a moment before answering. "I think Dixie and my sister knew they were being followed and tied their horses here. They went the rest of the way to the mine on foot."

"And these three horses?"

"They were also tied or being held by one of the followers. For some reason, they broke away and that's why their reins are broken. Horses find other horses to bunch up with when they are confused or afraid."

Ruff looked up the mountainside. "How far to your father's gold mine?"

"Just over the top of this ridge," Mando answered. "We're less than a quarter of a mile from it."

Darby dismounted with his shotgun. "I hate walking uphill," he complained. "I think we need to move forward quickly but with considerable caution."

The others nodded with agreement.

Darby said, "Dolly, I want you to stay here with these horses and ..."

"I'll do nothing of the sort!" She patted the gun on her shapely hip. "These horses would just trample all over me if they got scared and had a mind to bolt and run. I feel much safer with you men and I want to find out what happened to those girls as much as any one of you."

The way she spoke left no doubt that trying to change Dolly's opinion was a waste of time. So, they all tied their horses, checked their weapons and began to climb up the steep trail to the top of the ridge. From the back of their horses it hadn't seemed like much of a hike, but once on the ground, Darby and Dolly, being a little stouter and considerably older, really found themselves huffing and puffing.

But at last they topped the ridge and looked down to see a terrible sight. Men lay scattered near the mouth of the mine, blown over backward. Their hair and faces were burned beyond recognition and their clothes were half torn from their bodies.

"Reba!" Mando shouted, running down to where rocks had been and where now there was only a fresh rockslide. "Dixie!"

Ruff hardly glanced at the bodies. "Was this where you dug the mouth of the tunnel?"

"Yes. There used to be rocks and some brush in front of it."

Darby glanced up at the mountainside. He could see that tons of loose rock and gravel had rained down the slope to bury what was undoubtedly the mine's opening.

"We need to move these rocks and gravel!" Darby shouted, grabbing a heavy rock and heaving it aside.

Ruff, Mando and even Dolly Beavers joined him. Without picks or shovels, it was a hard and dirty job. But with the four of them heaving rocks and gravel aside, they were making good progress...or so they hoped.

Suddenly, they heard a faint voice. "Ruff?"

They froze. "Dixie? Are you and Reba alright?"

"We're alive," came the reply followed by a racking cough. "But we're hurt."

"We digging as fast as we can," Ruff shouted.

"We're doing the same," Reba cried from inside the tunnel.

Two hours later, when Darby and Dolly were completely exhausted by the hard effort and the altitude, they broke through into the mine with a hole large enough for the young women to crawl through.

Dolly was crying with happiness and darn near smothered both girls who were coated with rock dust.

"How did you possibly survive?" Ruff finally managed to ask, still shaking his head in disbelief.

"Reba has a hell of a throwing arm," Dixie explained. "She hurled a stick of dynamite all the way from the dogleg to the opening of the mine. We saw it bounce into the men and then we don't remember anything more. We were shielded by the dogleg and knocked clear back into the cavern."

"I've *got* to work this into a future dime novel," Darby muttered.

Dixie took a deep breath and looked around in the bright sunlight. "Including the one I shot, I count three bodies. There were four men chasing us up this mountain."

"Then one must have been holding the horses and standing farther back when the blast went off," Mando said. "And when he saw what was left of his friends, he mounted up and ran off."

Ruff nodded. "That means he knows where your gold mine is to be found."

"Yes," Reba agreed. "The secret is out and there will be many men coming here. Maybe not for a while, but whoever got away will tell his friends and they'll come to take what is left of the vein of pure gold."

"I can track him," Mando decided, "then kill him."

"I'll go with you," Ruff said solemnly. "Those four men meant to kill Reba and my sister. I'm not going to let that pass."

"Then let's hike back and over the ridge and get our horses."

"Please bring back our horses too," Dolly pleaded. "Darby and I really haven't the strength to hike back to them."

"Done," Mando said, hurrying up the hillside with Ruff on his heels.

CHAPTER 21

Mando followed a narrow, winding trail higher into the Granite Mountains and he soon leaned back in his saddle and said, "This man we are following is going up to *Ida-heh,* the Dog Man's wikiup."

"I hope he didn't kill your Yavapai friend or his guard dogs," Ruff fretted.

Mando turned back around in his saddle and urged his weary horse to move even faster. Then, just a hundred yards from the wikiup, they heard the Yavapai guard dogs barking furiously.

Mando sent his horse galloping forward, drawing a pistol from his holster. The dogs went crazy and came racing out to confront the new danger.

Mando reined up and started calling to the pack of barking and snarling dogs. He spoke in Yavapai and his voice was almost sing-song until the huge leader of the pack stopped and with a low rumble in his throat warily watched the two new arrivals.

"I don't think we dare get off these horses," Ruff said nervously.

"You stay mounted. I know these dogs and they will remember the scent of me."

"If not, they'll tear your throat out."

Mando never stopped speaking to the pack and the leader's rumble gradually fell silent. Leading his horse slowly forward, Mondo approached the pack and then he stopped and extended the back of his hand to the leader who came forward, smelled his scent and then turned around and quickly trotted back to the wickiup.

"There's Marshal Judd!" Ruff shouted, pointing to the torn-up body half in and half out of the brush. One of the marshal's legs was missing. "My gawd, they ripped him to shreds!"

"I see that." Mando walked slowly forward. When he came to the entrance to the wikiup, the dogs again began barking and growling. Speaking to the dogs he paused, then disappeared inside.

Ruff waited not knowing what to expect. After several minutes, Mando appeared carrying the body of a thin old Indian.

"Is he dead?"

Mando nodded. "There are four pups inside. They growled at me when I went in but then they started licking my hand. *Ida-heh* was shot dead by Marshal Judd. He probably came acting like a friend, but when he killed *Ida-heh,* the dogs knew he was an enemy and attacked."

"Helluva way to die," Ruff said quietly. "What do we do now?"

"We bury Ida-heh and leave."

"And his grown dogs?"

"We take the pups and raise them. If the mother of the pups and the others come with us, we will have many huge dogs to feed who will learn to protect us as well as the Thoroughbreds, chickens and goats."

Ruff stared at the menacing pack of dogs. The two males had to weigh 120 or 130 pounds each and the pair of females weren't all that much smaller. They looked more like wolves than dogs ... but there was something a little different about them ... something in the eyes, maybe.

"Dolly wanted a large dog ... or two. And we wanted a few ourselves." Ruff cautiously dismounted. "But ..."

"It will work out as it should," Mando told him while carrying the old Indian's body out to the edge of the yard and gently laying it down.

And then, the half-breed began to sing what Ruff Ballou figured was an ancient Yavapai Death Song.

AUTHOR'S NOTE

In 1975 I was an economist for the State of Nevada living in Carson City. I had great job with nice benefits, but I was bored crunching numbers. Five years earlier I'd taken an adult creative writing course in Reno taught by a wonderful old Professor Emeritus from the University of Oklahoma. Dr. Paul Eldridge had a devoted following of writers and the same students went semester after semester to his weekly evening classes. In truth, it was almost like a writing club, only it had someone who really knew how to teach writing.

After a few semesters, I confessed to Dr. Eldridge that I had a dream of becoming a full-time novelist. He told me to write in a genre that I liked. At the time, I was reading a lot of westerns, and I had owned, trained and showed horses throughout my youth. I had also known some real "Old Timers" and loved to listen to their true stories. And so, in 1971 I wrote my first western novel around my full-time economist's job. I thought at the time that first western novel was outstanding ... but of course it wasn't and it was rejected by every western publisher in New York City.

Set back by this failure I soon started another western and then another ... four years and four novels, *all rejected.* But I could see that my writing was improving with every western and I thought, *if I keep on improving then sooner or later, some editor will have to buy my story.*

I don't really know if that would have happened had not the Western Writers of America chosen Carson City for its 1975 Annual Convention. Although I didn't quality for professional membership, I wrote to the legendary western novelist Nelson Nye and asked if I could attend and help out. Nelson immediately wrote back inviting me to attend saying something like, *"Anyone who is stubborn enough to write four rejected westerns and is working on fifth ought to be invited for that reason alone!"*

I was as nervous and filled with anticipation as I could possibly be when the convention began. And I did help out however I could, even including borrowing someone's big Cadillac convertible with the top down to drive to the Reno airport to pick up well-known authors. On that trip, Western Writers of America's president and immensely talented writer, Jeanne Williams, was sitting on the front seat with me and we struck up a friendship that still continues over forty-five years later.

Soon after the convention, I got a letter from Doubleday Books saying they were going to publish *THE DERBY MAN* and give me an advance against royalties of $1,750.00! I was so thrilled I was ready to quit my economist job and probably would have if my wife hadn't offered wise counsel. Darby Buckingham was an off-beat character to be sure. Almost a year earlier when I still hadn't gotten published, I'd stomped through snow to watch *HIGH PLAINS DRIFTER* starring Clint Eastwood. I really like Clint Eastwood's acting and movies, but I did not care for that one. So when I left the movie house, I walked, lost in thought thinking that, *Gary, if you can't sell a "traditional western" with the main character being tall, fast with a gun, narrow at the hip and wide at the shoulder, then why not create a character that is exactly the opposite?*

And so, the idea of Darby Buckingham was born. He would be the most famous dime novelist of his day, slightly overweight, definitely past his prime and he couldn't shoot a gun or ride a horse. Anything else? Well, I gave him a derby hat and a wonderful and adoring girlfriend named Dolly Beavers. In the years to follow I sent Darby Buckingham all over the West looking for stories that *THE DERBY MAN* could use to feed his voracious army of readers.

My "break out" story, *THE DERBY MAN,* was a very successful novel. Critics hailed it and readers loved Darby and Dolly. Over the next few years, I wrote eight more *THE DERBY MAN* novels that were printed in many languages and allowed me to finally quit my well-paying but unfulfilling "economist day job."

I came to love Darby Buckingham and Dolly Beavers and I knew them so well I could anticipate their every word and move. They were interesting, very different and humorous characters having great adventures.

Having a family to support I wrote hard and fast and created many more western series like the *THE MEDICINE WAGON* and *RAILS WEST.* Every June we would meet at wherever the Western Writers Convention happened to be and Frank Roderus and I roomed together to swap story ideas and meet with western editors. During those years and right up to today, I have made a lot of wonderful writers and friends like Jory Sherman, Jeanne Williams, Glendon Swarthout, Laura Ashton, Fred Grove, Mike Bray, Irene Bennet Brown, Gary Challender, Dusty Richards, Frank Roderus, Preston Lewis, Doug Hirt, Matt Braun and the beloved and hugely admired Elmer Kelton.

In 1992 I created what was probably my most popular western series, *THE HORSEMEN.* It started at a famous Tennessee horse ranch called Wildwood Farm owned by the Ballou Family. It carried the survivors of that family and their magnificent Thoroughbreds to the West on dangerous and exciting adventures. They were always being pursued as traitors because they would not give the last few of their famous horses to be slaughtered on the bloody Civil War battlefields.

Because I had graduated from Cal Poly, Pomona, California in Animal Science and had owned, trained and ridden horses, I felt very comfortable writing about those wonderful animals.

THE HORSEMEN Series ran for five novels and

after I finished, I was asked by many fans to continue with the saga. But I'd moved on to big historical novels. I was blessed to work as lead writer on Jory Sherman's outstanding *RIVERS WEST* series as well as creating a *NATIONAL PARK* historical series that sent me to four of the most majestic National Parks in America.

Now, as I write this AUTHOR'S NOTE at the end of *THE HORSEMEN & THE DERBY MAN,* I realize that I still enjoy the challenge and process of writing a good western while developing interesting characters. Perhaps I will write more of this combination of Darby Buckingham, Dolly Beavers, the half-Cherokees, Ruff, Dixie, and Houston Ballou, and two interesting and new characters, Mando and Reba Parker, who are part Yavapai.

Time will tell.

Gary McCarthy in Arizona

A LOOK AT: THE HORSEMEN SERIES

SPUR AWARD WINNING AUTHOR OF THE DERBY MAN SERIES INTRODUCES A FAMILY HAUNTED BY THE CIVIL WAR...

After the Civil War devastates their home, the Ballous, a Tennessee horse breeding family, relocate and start anew in the West where their new neighbors could become lasting friends or tomahawk-toting enemies.

Lucas Ballou and his family share a love of wild horses with their Comanche neighbors, but the brutal Kiowa threaten their new start on the Texas frontier.

The Horsemen Omnibus includes books 1-5 of the action-packed western series!

AVAILABLE NOW ON AMAZON

ABOUT AUTHOR

Gary McCarthy is the author of fifteen published American historical and thirty-four westerns novels. In 1993, his "THE GILA RIVER" won the Western Writers of America's Spur Award as the best historical paperback novel of that year and "RIVER THUNDER" won the 2009 Western Writers of America's Spur Award for Best Audio Book. His 1991 "RUSSIAN RIVER" California historical novel and 2003 Arizona Western novel "RESTITUTION" were Spur Award Finalists. In 2019, he was awarded the Life Achievement Peacemaker Award by the Western Fictioneers. McCarthy received widespread recognition for his extremely well researched novels relating to our NATIONAL PARKS and his highly popular OUR AMERICAN WEST VOL. 1-4 SERIES. He is the creator of the THE DERBY MAN and the THE HORSEMEN SERIES. McCarthy has also worked on other successful series including RIVERS WEST, GUNSMOKE, RAILS WEST and the longest running series of them all...LONGARM.

He has also written three Script Stories based on his New York Published novels. The author is well suited to writing about the American West; he grew up with horses and received a B.S. degree in Animal Science and an M.S. in Economics from the University of Nevada. Before becoming a full time novelist, McCarthy was employed as an economist. He is very interested in Native American cultures, especially the Navajo, Hualapai and Hopi and historical preservation of southwestern western archaeological sites. McCarthy had been president of two Rotary Clubs and served on many community boards. Gary McCarthy has over five million books in print and resides in Arizona with his wife, Jane. He enjoys hiking and horseback riding in the Grand Canyon Rim Country when he is not traveling the Southwest in search of new stories upon which to base his next novel.

www.ingramcontent.com/pod-product-compliance
Lightning Source LLC
LaVergne TN
LVHW030919080826
845145LV00013B/2972

* 9 7 8 1 6 4 7 3 4 9 8 5 1 *